RUSHED

ALEATHA ROMIG

NEW YORK TIMES BESTSELLING AUTHOR

The Coopers Series Book Two

By New York Times bestselling author Aleatha Romig

COPYRIGHT AND LICENSE INFORMATION

RUSHED

The Coopers Series, book two

INTERCEPTED - Coopers book one - Coming February 2026

NAUGHTY AND NICE - A Brutal Vows Holiday Novella

Marriage of convenience, Mafia/cartel romance, romantic suspense, friends to lovers, he falls first, strong heroine, possessive hero, dangerous romance

FEAR OF FLAMES - A Romantic Thriller

Suspense, Crime, Corruption, Protective hero, Strong heroine, Thriller, Mystery, Romance, Curvy heroine, dangerous romance

DEFENDING LOVE - Standalone Novel

A steamy, high-stakes, romantic suspense with body-guard vibes, second chances, and all the feels—set in the same world as the Sinclair Duet

TO HAVE AND TO HOLD - Brutal Vows, book five - March 2025

Arranged marriage, Mafia/cartel, enemies to lovers, age-gap, he falls first, protective hero, Romeo and Juliet vibes, dangerous romance

QUEENS AND MONSTERS - Brutal Vows, book four - January 2025

Arranged marriage, Mafia/cartel, alpha hero, virgin

heroine, touch her and die, family saga, he falls first, posses-sive hero, sheltered heroine, dangerous romance

BOUND BY A PROMISE – Brutal Vows, book three - October 2024

Arranged marriage, age-gap, forbidden, Mafia/cartel dangerous stand-alone romance

ONE STRING – July 2024

Aleatha's Lighter Ones - Second-chance, enemies-to-lovers, fake-date, little-sister's-best-friend, forbidden, stand-alone contemporary romance

TILL DEATH DO US PART- Brutal Vows, book two - June 2024

Arranged marriage, enemies to lovers, Mafia/cartel, he falls first, stand-alone, dangerous romance

NOW AND FOREVER – Brutal Vows, book one - May 2024

Arranged marriage, age-gap, Mafia/cartel stand-alone romance

For a complete list of all Aleatha Romig's works, turn to BOOKS BY ALEATHA at the end of this novel.

Cooper:
A skilled craftsperson who makes or repairs wooden barrels, casks, and tubs.

Lexington, Kentucky:
Gateway city on the Kentucky Bourbon Trail.

Dedication and Inspiration

To my readers who are willing to one-click my books even when you're promised a jaw-dropping cliffhanger. I love your support and dedication to my imaginary friends. Thank you for always reading, reviewing, and recommending. Thank you for being Aleatha'd.

A special dedication to the Seattle Seahawks, the winners of Super Bowl LX. Such as is the case with my beloved Indianapolis Colts, the 2025-26 Seahawks has a female CEO/owner. Congratulations to Jody Allen, and the other women making their names known in this testosterone-filled business.

SYNOPSIS:

From the bestselling author of *Infidelity* and *Sin* comes an addictive football romance series filled with power plays, forbidden passion, and jaw-dropping twists.

He was her past. Now he might cost her the future.

I was born into a football dynasty built on power, money, and secrets.

Now those secrets are unraveling.

The truth about my family threatens everything from the franchise to the locker room. Allies I trusted have their own agendas. And in the NFL's ruthless good ol' boys club, there's no mercy for a woman who dares to challenge the league's power structure.

This isn't just football.

It's an empire. It's a legacy. It's war.

With the franchise and my future on the line, there's only one man I might be able to trust.

Fin—Griffin Graham.

Elite NFL quarterback. The new face of the team.

My past. My weakness. My second chance.

Our chemistry still burns hotter than game-day lights. But in a professional football world ruled by contracts, media scrutiny, and billion-dollar reputations, falling for the star quarterback again could destroy everything we're fighting to protect.

With more than our season on the line, I'm forced to choose a side.

Will it be the right choice?

Have you been Aleatha'd?

Rushed is book two of *The Coopers*, a second-chance sports romance wrapped in betrayal, dynasty drama, and high-stakes romantic suspense set in the seductive, cutthroat world of professional football. **RUSHED ends on a cliffhanger—an unforgettable Aleatha blindside.**

The Coopers is a four-book football romance saga following one explosive couple, beginning with **INTERCEPTED**, which must be read prior to **RUSHED.** Perfect for fans of the ruthless tension of *Succession* and the dark, aching obsession of *Wuthering Heights*.

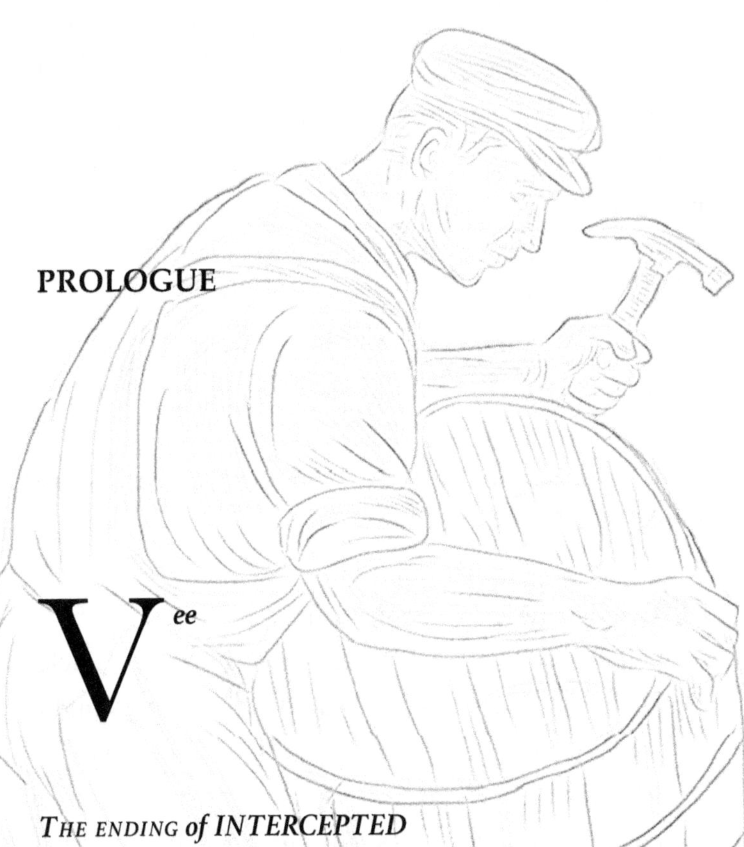

PROLOGUE

V*ee*

T*HE* ENDING *of* INTERCEPTED

I CONTINUED RIDING the elevator down to the garage. Once I was on my way, I called Jen. She answered on the first ring.

"Hi," I said, "are you at Maker's Mark?"

"I am. Do you need anything?"

"I was checking to see if you needed me. I'm on my way, but I'm going to stop by my dad's office before going to mine."

"You have emails you probably want to see before

the executive meeting," she said. "Oh, and Mr. Darin Marsh called for you about five minutes ago. I told him you weren't in yet."

"Uncle Darin? I wonder what he wanted."

"He didn't say."

"I'll give him a call, and I'll be in after I talk with Dad."

"Sounds good," Jen said.

I disconnected the line and spoke to my car. "Make phone call. Call Uncle Darin."

"Calling Uncle Darin," the car replied.

His line rang and rang. After the fourth or fifth ring, the call went to his voicemail. I spoke. "Uncle Darin, Jen said you called. I should be to Maker's Mark in fifteen minutes or less."

My GPS routed me through city streets, avoiding the major interstates. I spent the rest of the drive rehearsing how I would tell Dad my news. I was wrestling with blurting it out or easing into it. By the time I walked into Maker's Mark, I was pretty sure blurting was what would happen.

"Ms. Hubbard," Tricia, one of the front receptionists, said.

"Good morning, Tricia."

"Maeve, you're wanted in Mr. Hubbard's office."

I stood straighter. "I was planning on going there."

"They're waiting for you."

My forehead furrowed. "Who is?"

She shook her head. "I don't know for sure."

"Okay, I'm on my way."

My heart thumped in my chest as I made my way to the complex of executive offices. All I could think of was that whoever was waiting wanted to confront me about me and Fin.

Who knows?

Did Lip or Leigh let it slip?

Why were they making a big deal out of this?

I clenched my teeth at the sight of Grant. Of course, he'd make more out of me and Fin than necessary.

Stepping into Dad's office suite, I was caught short by the sight of everyone on the executive committee. They all turned to me.

"Is this..." I began to say when I realized the only person missing.

"Vee," Aunt Rachel said, with tears in her eyes.

"What's going on?" I managed to say as a lump formed in my throat. "Where's Dad?"

"Vee," Uncle Darin said. His eyes were also red. "There was an accident this morning on 64."

"An accident?" It wasn't making sense.

"A semi-truck..." Grant said.

"Vee," Aunt Rachel said, reaching for my hand. "Reid was pronounced dead at the scene."

I shook my head. "No. No. There's a mistake."

"We need to talk," Uncle Darin said. "Reid was in

the middle of changing his will. He hadn't completed the change yet, but he was going to."

Gripping the back of a chair, I willed my knees to keep standing. The room was spinning, I couldn't focus. "What are you saying?"

Uncle Darin's gaze met mine. "Reid didn't want the Coopers to go one hundred percent to you."

My neck straightened. "My father is gone, and you're talking about the Coopers?"

"As his will stands, you're now the owner and CEO. What do you plan on doing?"

"I'm not doing anything until I see my dad."

CHAPTER 1

Vee

I looked around the room in astonishment—my uncle, aunt, and cousins. These people were my family, my *father's* family. And yet, instead of showing concern and shock at our terrible loss, they were focused on the ownership of the Coopers. "Where is he?"

Aunt Rachel led me to the chair across from my father's desk—the desk that used to be his. I sat as she took a seat in the chair to my side. "The state police said an ambulance would transport Reid to the Fayette County Coroner's Office."

Her words were muted as if I were listening through an old telephone or to a scratchy vinyl album. "I-I... I don't know what to do." I looked up. "Do we need to call someone?" My questions disappeared into a void. Oh God, Daphne. My next question came louder. "Has Daphne been told?"

Aunt Rachel nodded. "The police went to their home first. Daphne had to be woken up. The detective said she was in shock and asked him to contact Darin. Darin called your office as soon as we heard."

I began to nod. "Yes, I remember. Jen told me he called." I looked up at my uncle. "I called you back and it went to voicemail."

"We didn't want to inform you while you were driving," he said.

Because I couldn't handle it.

That's what he'd decided. I would be too emotional.

He was right about my emotions. They were racing through my circulation, filling me with an unexplainable sense of loss. While falling to the floor in a fetal position and sobbing until I couldn't sob anymore was what my mind and body wanted to do, it wasn't the person Reid Hubbard raised me to be. I squared my shoulders. "The coroner's office..." I tried to think. "Will they let me see him?"

"They requested a family member to identify Reid's...to identify him," Uncle Darin said.

I stood suddenly. "Wait. They're not sure." A seed of hope burst within my chest. "Maybe it's not him. Maybe they made a mistake." My gaze went to the closed door, wishing for my dad to materialize. I could almost picture him sauntering through the front office, greeting his staff, and smiling with his green eyes shining.

The gripping of my heart and the heaviness in my chest told me the police weren't wrong. It was wrong of me to have false hope.

My temples pounded as I pushed the image away, straightened my shoulders, and turned to Uncle Darin. "I'll go to the coroner's office."

He shook his head. "Vee, you don't have to do that. Daphne asked me. I'll do it."

Of course Daphne wouldn't do it herself.

I stood. "I'm going. We can go together, but I'm going."

"Rachel?" he asked.

"Vee, do you want me to come along?"

In the years after my mother left and before Daphne, Rachel was the stable female in my life. Even after Daphne, Rachel was my go-to. While my single father assured me that I was loved, there were girl things and questions that arose. Without hesitation, my aunt filled the void. "No. I need to do this. You, Grant, and Lip can take care of things here." Suddenly, I had the realization that this tragedy affected many more people beyond our bubble. "Royce and the coaches. Have they been told?"

"No one has," Uncle Darin said. "We needed to reach you first."

My mind was a cyclone of thoughts. "The press." I turned to Grant. "As vice president of communications, you and I need to decide on a statement." Grant began to talk, but I continued. "We first need to inform Royce and the coaches. Our team should hear this news from us, not from a news outlet."

Lip looked up from his phone. "TMZ just broke the news."

The urgency enveloping us gave me strength. "Uncle Darin, we'll go to the coroner's office after I address the team."

Grant reached for my arm. "Let Dad do that."

Wrenching my arm back, I walked to the office door. "Bre," I called to Dad's personal assistant. When she met my gaze, I went on, "Please contact Royce Beasley, Coach Tilson, Andrew Pratt, and Darius Brown. Ask them to move all the players into the large viewing room. I'll be addressing them in a few minutes. First, I need to speak to Royce and the coaches. We can meet in Royce's office."

"Right away, Vee." She furrowed her forehead. "Is there something wrong?"

Pressing my lips together, I nodded. "There is." My thoughts expanded. The coaching staff and players needed to be told, but there were roughly another seventy-five employees currently in Maker's Mark Football Center. "Bre, instead of the film room, ask Royce to send the players to the indoor practice facility." I turned around to Grant. "Can you have the PA system turned on?"

My cousin nodded.

I turned back to Bre. "I need all employees in the building to join the team and coaches in the indoor practice facility in ten minutes. No phones."

"Yes."

I turned back to everyone in the office. "The players should be watching film. Hopefully, no one is scrolling on their phone."

Uncle Darin shook his head. "Tilson doesn't tolerate that."

"Good. His rule may avoid a panic."

My thoughts raced. If TMZ was talking, the Coopers needed to get out ahead of the rumors. "How did they identify him...the police?"

Uncle Darin was the one to answer. "License plate. The car was registered to Reid Hubbard. They also saw his identification."

I let out a sigh. "There wasn't a mistake?"

"No, Vee. No mistake."

"Grant," I said, "the Coopers need to make a statement. We can't get ahead of TMZ, but we can stop the rumor mill. Make it simple: The Hubbard family and Lexington Coopers..." When he didn't move, I hardened my tone. "Write this down."

"Vee, you're not in charge."

"Right now I am. Write it down."

Grant pulled his phone from the inside pocket in his sports coat. "The Hubbard family and the Lexington Coopers..." he repeated.

"Have been notified," I began, "of the untimely death of Reid Hubbard, 65, CEO of the Lexington Coopers. Our family asks for privacy at this difficult time. We will share more information once more is known." I met his gaze. "Don't release the statement until I'm in front of everyone."

Grant looked from me to his father. When Uncle Darin nodded, Grant agreed.

Aunt Rachel reached for my hand. "I'm going with you down to Royce's office and the practice field."

"We need to hurry."

As the two of us traversed the long amber hallway, I thought about how much more familiar I was with the football operations side than I'd been at the beginning of preseason. It wasn't only the building, but the people. Tears prickled my eyes as I said a silent thank-you to Dad for encouraging me to learn more about the football side of the franchise.

"Why didn't Grandpa Carroll leave half of the Coopers to you?"

Aunt Rachel blinked rapidly and pursed her lips. "This isn't the time."

"Was it because you're female?"

"It seems the logical answer."

"But it's not logical."

"It was nearly twenty-five years ago," she replied. "Things have changed. And even though Reid wasn't obligated to include me, he made sure Darin and I were a part of the Coopers. It's a family business. It has been since our dad bought the team. I know he'd want it to stay that way."

My feet quit moving. "Are you, or anyone" —my volume rose— "seriously concerned that I will cut any of my family out of the franchise?"

"Vee, we have time for that in the future. Right now—"

Inhaling, I nodded. "You're right."

Together, we approached Royce Beasley's office. Again, I tried to fill my lungs. Our general manager was standing inside near his desk with an irritated expression. Our head coach, Tilson, offensive coordinator, Drew Pratt, and defensive coordinator, Darius Brown were also present.

They turned as we grew nearer.

"What is this about? We have work we should be doing," Royce said as he gestured around. "All of us."

I nodded once. "Gentlemen, there's no easy way to tell you what I need to say, except to say it." My heart thumped against my breastbone as I maintained my posture. "The Kentucky State Police informed us of an accident on 64."

The four men were now staring at me.

"My father was killed."

The room filled with collective gasps.

"Vee," Drew said, taking a step toward me. "Are they sure? Are you all right?"

I backed up a half step. I couldn't look into Drew's concerned gaze. I had to maintain the walls I'd hastily constructed around my emotions and heart, the ones that would allow me to do whatever needed to be done —to be Reid Hubbard's daughter. Swallowing, I spoke to the room. "Uncle Darin and I will be going to the coroner's office soon to make a positive ID. However, when the police spoke to Darin, they were certain of Dad's identity. We don't have a lot of information yet. Nevertheless, we decided it was best for the team and others who are a part of the Coopers to hear it from us first."

"This is terrible news," Royce said, looking at Tilson. "Everything was going our way. Now what?"

"We continue," I said. "My dad wouldn't want it any other way."

"I'm assuming," Royce said, "Darin Marsh will assume Reid's responsibilities as CEO for the time being."

"That's incorrect. I am now the owner and CEO of the Coopers."

CHAPTER 2

Vee

Silence hung in the air. If any one of these men wanted to challenge my authority, I was prepared to meet them head-on. Aunt Rachel was the one to speak. "Vee will have the full support of me and my husband. The Coopers will remain our top priority." The tension eased. "We should go to the practice field."

"Are the players in the indoor facility?" I asked.

Coach Tilson was the one to answer. "They should all be there, Ms. Hubbard."

"Vee," I corrected. "The same name I had yesterday I have today."

"What can we do?" Drew asked.

"What you always do." I met each man's eyes. "You were right, Royce. You were right about things going our way and you were right about Graham. If my father taught me anything, it was that he surrounded himself with the best of the best. I have no intentions of changing that."

Changing the venue of my announcement to the practice field was a good move. Uncle Darin, Grant, and Lip were already on the field with a microphone. The stands were filling with players and Coopers' staff. The sound of heavy footsteps on the aluminum bleachers echoed throughout the facility. In the film room, I would be able to see each face and each expression. From the practice field, I could look out at the group without zeroing in on individuals.

I willed myself not to find Fin.

As soon as Grant passed me the microphone, I was caught in Fin's blue stare. His expression was shared by those around him, one of curiosity and uncertainty. I pulled my gaze away from Fin's and focused on the crowd.

"Thank you for coming in here on short notice and disrupting your day," I said into the microphone, my voice projecting through the facility. "This morning, after my arrival to Maker's Mark, I was informed of an accident on 64." I inhaled. "We don't have specific information, but we know with certainty that my father, Reid Hubbard, was killed in that crash."

I waited as mouths went agape. A few people

covered their faces with their hands. Gasps and whispers filled the air.

"I—we, Dad's family, wanted you to hear the news from us. TMZ has already announced his passing in an unconfirmed newsbreak. I can only imagine that soon Maker's Mark Football Center will be crawling with reporters looking for the scoop on the story." I looked at Grant and then back to the crowd. "Our statement is that we, the family, appreciate privacy. You, every one of you sitting or standing here, are part of our family."

Heads nodded.

"Our security won't allow the journalists to enter the facility, but I would assume you will be questioned. Sports reporters are probably currently leaving messages on your phones. I'm not going to dictate what you say. I ask that you plead for the privacy we requested." I waited as the news settled in. "However, I want everyone in here to know I'm also asking for something else. I'm asking that we carry on the season we began. The Coopers will not miss the game next Sunday in Las Vegas. Practices will continue. The coaches will continue to coach. Please remember my father with a smile and continue to strive for the best. Reid Hubbard believed in you, each of you and the collective you. He told me more than once that he believed this was our year to win the Super Bowl. I believe that too. I know that whether the season ends with a ring or without, my father was proud and honored to have each of you in his life."

To my shock and surprise, one by one, people began to stand and clap.

The walls around my emotions began to crumble. Tears streamed down my cheeks, ones I hoped weren't visible from a distance. I swallowed the sob building in my chest. I lifted my hand. "Thank you for listening. Now, let's do our best for my dad, Reid Hubbard."

"Ms. Hubbard. Vee." Hands shot upward.

"I'm sorry," I said. "I'm not taking any questions at this time. I've briefed Mr. Beasley and the coaches. You may ask your questions of them. I need to be going." I handed the microphone back to Grant.

"The Coopers' statement went out as you began to speak," he said. "You're right about the journalists. You and Dad should get out of here while you can."

"How close can the journalists get?"

Grant clenched his teeth. His nostrils flared. "I'll speak with security. We should be able to keep them outside the parking lot. I'll have security close the gates and post guards outside."

"Thank you."

The players and staff were quietly climbing down and off the metal stands as condolences filled my ears. When I turned to leave, I was met with the blue stare I'd awakened to this morning.

Concern emanated through Fin's expression. My

first instinct was to shake my head, letting him know I couldn't speak to him, not now. However, before I shook my head, I feigned a smile and nodded toward the exit.

Fin nodded in response.

The crowd moved through the doors, scattering in different directions. I took the less traveled path—a turn to the right, the direction leading me toward the training and medical center. Sidestepping, I ducked into an alcove, hoping Fin followed my lead.

I heard his footsteps before he passed. I had a quick glimpse of his determined saunter, squared shoulders, and clenched jaw as I called out in a hushed whisper.

"Fin."

He spun toward me and scanned the hallway, before entering the privacy of the alcove. Fin's strong arms wrapped me in his embrace, pulling me against his hard chest. "Vee, I'm so sorry." His words reverberated from him to me as his heart beat beneath his button-down shirt.

Nodding, I swallowed the sob attempting an escape and blinked away the tears. As I pushed away from his hold, our hands found one another's. Stoically, I met his sympathetic gaze. "I don't want to shut you out. But right now, I need to concentrate—"

"Don't shut me out," he interrupted. "You shouldn't be alone."

"I'm just..." My nostrils flared and my voice quivered. "If I give in for a second, I'm not sure I can remember how to be strong."

His warm lips kissed my forehead. "You're fucking strong, standing in front of all of us like that."

"I'm not strong. I'm numb."

"I want to wrap you in my arms and go back to this morning."

Blinking away the onslaught of tears, I pressed my lips together and nodded. "I'd do anything to go back. I'd call Dad and ask him to meet me for coffee. Change his route..." I shook my head. "I-I can't think about it."

Fin squeezed my hands. "What do you have to do... now?"

"Uncle Darin and I are going to the county coroner's office. They need a positive ID."

"But you said—"

"I said we're certain it was Dad. It was his car and the state police found his identification. They still want someone to make a visual confirmation."

"I'll go with you."

"No," I protested with a shake of my head. "Thank you. I love you for wanting to go. You're needed here. You're starting in Vegas." My lips curled upward. "Remember last game when the crowd was chanting your name? That's what you can do for Dad and for me; kick the Raiders' ass."

"Tonight?"

"I'm going to my place."

"I want to be with you."

Pressing my lips together, I inhaled, too uncertain of anything to argue. "Then it's a good thing you have a keycard." I brushed my lips over his. "I need to go."

"Vee, I'm so sorry."

Fin held on to my hand until I walked away. The loss of our connection amplified my solitude. The pounding in my temples returned, growing louder as I acknowledged concerned players and staff, forced my emotions to stay locked away, and made my way to Uncle Darin's office.

Without prelude, I passed his assistant and pushed open his door.

Uncle Darin and Aunt Rachel turned toward me.

"What the hell happened to you? You were with us and then you weren't," he asked.

"I'm here now. Let's go."

CHAPTER 3

Vee

The traffic through Lexington was stop-and-go as Uncle Darin drove us across the city. Our destination, the Fayette County Coroner's Office, was roughly twenty minutes away from Maker's Mark Football Center on a good day. Today, it seemed as if we were moving in slow motion and hitting red at most of the stoplights. Conversation was at a minimum as we both navigated our thoughts. About ten minutes into the drive, I noticed that the GPS was taking us by the University of Kentucky campus.

Memories from over fifteen years ago flooded my mind. During my junior year of high school, Dad took me on multiple college visits around the country.

University of Michigan had one of the top sports management programs. University of Florida and Texas A&M were also highly ranked. As far as private universities were concerned, Rice University in Houston, Texas, was the Ivy League of options.

Together, the two of us traveled to and from different universities. For farther away destinations such as Texas, California, and Florida, we took the team plane. For the relatively closer options, Dad drove. The two of us piled in his car and headed north, five hours to Ann Arbor, Michigan, and six hours to Chicago.

I thought I'd like a bigger city. I didn't.

While I'd managed to keep my father's identity hidden from many classmates at the University of Kentucky, upon my various applications, the name Reid Hubbard stood out like a neon sign. We were often met by top counselors for private tours of the university. After each visit was over, Dad and I would find a local pizza parlor—never a chain. Together, we sat, ate greasy, cheesy pizza, and talked about the pros and cons of the recent location.

It might be hard to believe that a man with as much responsibility as my father would take two or three days at a time to travel the country with his only daughter, but he did. After all the visits, I narrowed the search down to University of Michigan and University of Kentucky. The Kentucky program wasn't as renowned; nevertheless, in hindsight, there was part of the seventeen-year-old girl who wasn't ready to be over three hundred miles away from her father.

I brushed an unwanted tear from my cheek.

Despite my choosing a university close to home, Dad wanted me to have the full college experience. That meant dorm life during my freshman year. The day Dad moved me into my freshman dorm, he gave me a hug and told me he was happy with my choice. Though he was surrounded by college freshmen, none recognized the man in blue jeans, a shirt, and sneakers as the owner of the Lexington Coopers. The next three years of my undergraduate study, I shared an apartment with Emma. She was from Indiana and kept my secret throughout our under-grad journey.

I blinked away the tears as Uncle Darin passed by what used to be the New Commonwealth Stadium, currently Kroger Field—the place where the Kentucky Wildcats played football. Despite my attempt at anonymity, Dad attended many of the UK home foot-ball games while I worked with the team. He didn't do so with fanfare—most likely the reason Daphne rarely accompanied him. No, I later learned that Dad purchased season tickets in the stands. Blending in with the other parents, he quietly watched me on the sidelines.

"Vee," Uncle Darin asked, "are you sure you can do this?"

This.

The question and the slowing of the vehicle brought me back to the present as I eyed the building before us. I didn't know what I was expecting, but a worn-down, one-story brick building painted gray with two flags and a large sign was not it. I turned to Uncle Darin. "Are you sure this is where they brought him?"

Uncle Darin pulled his car up to the building and shut off the engine. "This is it." His tone was somber. "It's all right if you've changed your mind."

A single tear slid down his cheek that he didn't try to hide.

"Neither one of us wants to be here," I said. "I can't believe he's really gone."

"But you can see him after they do whatever they do. This could traumatize—"

"There wasn't anything Dad wouldn't do for me. I'm going to do this for him." Instead of waiting for a reply, I turned and opened the passenger side door. The overcast mid-October sky was various shades of gray. The clouds seemed to amplify our somber moods. An autumn breeze rustled the orange and yellow leaves in the nearby trees. Grabbing ahold of the black railing, I climbed the steps to the glass door.

The three steps felt as if I were climbing Mount Everest. Each step was more difficult than the last. As I reached for the door handle, the dizzying sense of oxygen deprivation took over, and black spots danced before my eyes. Filling my lungs became paramount.

After I gulped a few deep breaths, Uncle Darin materialized at my side. He too had made it to the summit. Together, we entered the plain front office. Nothing registered. There was nothing special about the interior.

Uncle Darin spoke to the woman behind the counter. "Darin Marsh and Maeve Hubbard. We were told by Detective Pelt of the state police that my brother-in-law and Vee's father, Reid Hubbard, was brought here earlier today."

"Yes, Mr. Marsh." She nodded toward me. "Ms. Hubbard. My name is Angela and I'm sorry for your loss." She stood and gestured to the end of the counter. "Please come with me."

My shoes remained glued to the cracked old flooring as my heart rate accelerated and my hands began to shake. "Are you...taking us...to him?"

"First," Angela said, "I'll take you to a private room. Robert Gordon is the crisis counselor on staff today. He'll be in shortly and explain everything to you."

Uncle Darin laid his hand in the small of my back. "Will you make it, Vee?"

I nodded, ungluing my shoes from the tile as the tears that could no longer be restrained streamed down my cheeks.

The room where we were led was nondescript, small, and sterile. We stepped inside. Taking a step away from my uncle's touch, I wrapped my arms around my midsection and looked around. A worn leather sofa sat against one wall opposite a table with three chairs. It was the kind of table with collapsible leaves. One was open, making the table an incomplete circle. When Angela closed the door, leaving Uncle Darin and I alone, I noticed two boxes of tissues. However, it was as if nothing truly registered.

The sofa was black.

A plastic plant sat on the windowsill.

The flowers in the vase on the table were silk.

"Vee, why don't you sit?" Uncle Darin asked.

"Have you" —I lowered my arms— "ever done this before?"

He took a seat at the table. "No."

I took the seat opposite my uncle.

Time moved in uneven increments.

We waited.

A strange concoction of sorrow, dread, and anticipation brewed within me, unlike anything I'd ever known. I wanted to go back in time, as I'd told Fin. While at the same time, I wanted to jump ahead, to have this in the past, not the present.

Looking around, I searched for a ticking clock. If this were a movie or television show, there would be a clock ticking. The only wall décor was an enlarged photograph with dark matting in a silver frame, hanging over the sofa. The picture was a close-up of leaves covered with water droplets. Beneath one leaf wrapped in what appeared to be a silk web was a white cocoon.

What an odd picture.

I jumped as the door opened.

CHAPTER 4

Vee

Robert Gordon, an older man, probably older than my dad or Uncle Darin, introduced himself as the crisis counselor. He had a deep, soothing voice, firm handshake, and odd aroma. His white hair was pulled tightly back into a low ponytail. The shirt and khaki pants beneath his white lab coat were wrinkled, and his dirty white tennis shoes seemed out of place.

A tense silence filled the air as Mr. Gordon took the third seat at the table. Laying an electronic tablet in the center of the table, he exhaled and spoke, "I'm very sorry for your loss..."

His words were kind and filled with practiced compassion, as if he was required to repeat them day after day. After some obligatory pleasantries, he showed us pictures and asked if we could identify them.

There was a picture of Dad's car, a new-model silver Porsche 911 Turbo Cabriolet. My stomach lurched. "It's his car," I confirmed. The top was down and the airbags inflated. I stared in disbelief at the crushed metal, shattered glass, and mangled side.

"The police explained the accident?" Mr. Gordon asked.

Uncle Darin nodded.

I didn't move, my focus on the picture.

Apparently, Mr. Gordon took my silence as permission to recount the report. "The police report states that at roughly 7:15 a.m. the accident occurred. The semi-truck driver claimed he didn't see Mr. Hubbard's car when he was forced to change lanes. While they're still studying the site, tire marks, and debris, it's believed Mr. Hubbard swerved to avoid the truck, becoming pinned between the truck and the side wall. The quick maneuver caused the truck's trailer to wobble. The driver tried to avoid a jack-knife situation. The size of your father's car..."

The breakfast Fin made earlier this morning was threatening to reappear. I lifted my hand. "Please stop."

Mr. Gordon changed the picture; however, it was another of the accident scene.

I shook my head. "The driver of the truck wasn't injured?"

"Not to my knowledge," he replied.

I looked toward Uncle Darin.

"They tested the truck driver's blood," Uncle Darin said, "and are checking his log to learn if he exceeded the acceptable hours driving. The results aren't in."

My dad was gone and it could be because some man didn't stop to rest or had illegal levels or illegal substances in his system. I couldn't think about that, not now.

Next, Mr. Gordon showed us pictures of Dad's personal belongings: his watch, his ID, his wedding ring, and the leather satchel he always carried back and forth to work. We identified each object as belonging to Dad.

This session was unbearably long as Mr. Gordon began asking more questions.

What was Dad's full name?

What was his date of birth?

Did we know his medical history?

Was he taking any medication?

Did he have a religious affiliation?

Did he have any tattoos?

What about scars?

"He had a scar on his forearm," I said. "It was from a dog bite when he was young."

The questions continued.

Uncle Darin and I answered what we could. For the first time I could recall, I wished for Daphne's presence. Surely, she knew more about Dad's health than either one of us.

"Mr. Hubbard's body will remain here until after the autopsy," Mr. Gordon said.

Blinking, I conjured the will to participate in the conversation around me. "Why do you want an autopsy? It was an accident, right?"

"In the case of fatal automobile accidents, the coroner often requires an autopsy."

"But you already know how he died."

"We only know the obvious."

I didn't know the ins and outs of an autopsy, but the idea of anyone desecrating Dad's body caused bile to churn in my stomach. "Can we object?"

"The family can refuse a private or hospital-requested autopsy, but unfortunately, not one ordered by the coroner."

"Will it...be noticeable...to us?" I was aware my question wasn't well stated. To be honest, I wasn't certain what I was asking.

"No, Ms. Hubbard. When we release your father's body to the funeral home and they'll prepare him for viewing, no one will be able to tell that an autopsy was performed."

"How long does all this take?" Uncle Darin asked.

"Typically, twenty-four to forty-eight hours. That is, of course, if the autopsy doesn't yield any unusual findings. Have you contacted a mortuary?"

My gaze went to Uncle Darin. This would be Daphne's call, not ours. I turned back to Mr. Gordon. "We'll let you know as soon as we've made the arrangements."

He nodded, adding information to his tablet. "We'll need to be contacted by the executor of Mr. Hubbard's estate."

Uncle Darin pulled a paper from the inside breast pocket of his suit coat. "Here's a copy of the paperwork you need. According to Mr. Hubbard's wishes, my wife and I are co-executors of his estate."

The information hit me with the force of a sledgehammer. "Dad planned for this?" I asked, dumbfounded.

"Not for *this*," Uncle Darin replied. "His will is outdated, but it stated what I just said."

"What else does it say? How outdated?"

Uncle Darin turned my way with a curt nod. "I tried to discuss this with you earlier." Before I could respond, he went on. "We can discuss it later."

Arguing at this juncture was beyond my current capability.

Mr. Gordon took the paperwork. "I'll need this information confirmed by the courts. After that—"

Unable to sit, I quickly stood. "Mr. Gordon, we came here today to see my father, not to answer a million questions. The rest of the legal issues can be discussed with my uncle and Dad's attorneys at a later time." Despite my assertive tone, I held tightly to my own hands to keep them from trembling. "I want to see my father."

Mr. Gordon nodded.

The odd time continuum moved forward. Again, the scenes weren't real. They were choppy, as if from a low-budget film with horrible lighting and terrible sound. My ears echoed with the tap of our shoes clipping along the hallway and bouncing off the cement-block walls. Mr. Gordon led us beyond multiple sets of doors. Each passage was colder than the one before.

I wasn't fully present.

If this was a dream, it was a nightmare I wanted to end.

Leaving my body, it was as if I were seeing the scene from above.

Mr. Gordon opened a door, one of many on a long wall. For some reason, they reminded me of oven doors. I had an irrational thought: it was too cold for ovens. He pulled out a long table containing a figure covered by a white sheet.

My body convulsed and tears streamed down my cheeks as I struggled to breathe.

Mr. Gordon donned a pair of blue gloves, the color standing out amongst the monochrome environment. After looking at us, he lowered the sheet to Dad's shoulders.

Unsuccessfully holding back the sobs, I stared

down at the face that had been my constant forever. Unbelievably, my lips curled. The sight wasn't gruesome. After the description of the accident, I had horrible images running through my mind. While Dad was pale, he looked like he had yesterday in the family suite.

A strangled laugh came from my throat. "He looks like he's sleeping. He's not gone. Wake him up."

Uncle Darin reached for my hand and spoke to Mr. Gordon. "That's him. That's Reid Hubbard."

Mr. Gordon's gaze came to me. "Ms. Hubbard?"

"Yes. It's him." I took my hand back and moved a half step closer. Staring down, my voice wobbled. "I love you, Dad."

In the sliver of time I stood over my father, a monumental shift occurred—the buckling of tectonic plates. Earthquakes, volcanic activity, and tsunamis were changing the topography of my life for eternity. Forever, I'd think of before and after.

Without resistance, I allowed Uncle Darin to lead me from the room, down the cold hallways, until we were once again outside. I gulped the fresh air like a dehydrated person guzzling water. Leaning on the black railing, I struggled to stand. The confirmation that my dad was gone was too much to bear, too heavy of a weight.

I was now in the after and going back wasn't an option.

As a fine mist of rain hit my cheeks, I looked up at the clouds and smiled. Even God was sad by this loss. The heavens were crying. I wasn't sure why the soft drizzle revived my strength, but it did. It was like the watering of dry, cracked soil—even when life didn't want to continue, it would.

With the rain mixing with my tears, I straightened my shoulders.

"We need to talk to Daphne," I said as I made my way to Uncle Darin's car. I put my hand on the door handle and stared across the roof. "I don't care what she wants. We need to make plans, and we need to make them today."

Uncle Darin nodded.

CHAPTER 5

Fin

The players in the offense film room were quiet after Vee's announcement. Drew Pratt was speaking, but the usual vigor was absent from his voice. Coach Garcia was present, listening and taking notes, yet saying very little. As the mood turned more somber and a palpable uneasiness penetrated the air, Pratt turned off the video. "We need to talk."

Every player in the room shifted in their chairs.

"I'm not sure what you're thinking," Pratt said. "I'd assume it's a lot like what I'm thinking. That's shock." He shook his head and inhaled. "Loss. Disbelief. I spoke with Reid after the game yesterday. No one expected this."

A few hands shot up into the air.

Pratt pointed to Ortiz, our running back. "Ms. Maeve said the season will go on. She said that's what Mr. Hubbard would want."

An attitude of consensus filled the room with hums.

"But who's going to take over Reid Hubbard's job?" Patel, our wide receiver, asked.

Pratt exhaled. "I don't want to speculate."

"The Coopers need to name someone," Patel said.

Pratt looked at Garcia and back to the room of players. "From what I know, in name that will be Ms. Hubbard."

The approving hum faded into sounds of discontent.

Pratt lifted his hand. "The Hubbards and Marshes have worked together for the best interest of the Coopers in the past. I don't see that changing. I don't want to add to the rumors of succession. I can only hope it's a smooth transition."

"Mr. Darin Marsh is the most qualified," Young, an offensive tackle, said.

"Mrs. Rachel Marsh has been with the team longer than her husband," Coach Garcia added in response.

"Grant Marsh has been here over eighteen years."

Opinions were spouted around the room.

"I know," Pratt said, quieting the noise, "we like to think that all there is to the Coopers is our part. That's not the case, and everyone here knows that. You know who else knows that?" He only paused for a moment. "Every single person in the executive wing. From Darin Marsh to Maeve Hubbard, they all know what it takes to keep a team like the Coopers going strong. Our job, gentlemen, is to do as Vee asked and play the game. Play hard. You have tomorrow off to rest. Spend the day mourning this tragedy. When we meet again on Wednesday, your focus, *our* focus is on Vegas—on beating the Raiders." He nodded toward where Dennison and I were sitting. "On Wednesday, we're welcoming Troy Dennison back to the practice field."

We all applauded.

Troy stood and bowed dramatically at the waist.

"And if you're wondering about Cody Simpson, well, Sean Lester from the defensive line is officially on the IR. That means, as Cody and I discussed this morning, he's still on the active roster."

I leaned forward and patted Simpson's shoulder.

"Fin will be starting Sunday in Vegas."

As he spoke about particulars, it was as if in those few minutes, our minds could forget the loss of the Coopers owner and CEO, the loss of Vee's father. We could remember that we were, first and foremost, teammates and players.

"Coach Tilson is waiting for us in the large film room," Pratt said.

"Glad you're going to be back in practice," I said to Dennison. "I'm ready to watch you control the field."

"Man, you've shown me some great moves over the last few weeks. It would be a lie if I said I'm content on the bench." He raised an eyebrow. "I'm cleared. Weights tomorrow?"

My first thought was of Vee. "I think I'm going to follow Pratt's advice and take tomorrow to give respect to a man I never really knew."

"Yeah, I didn't know him either." Dennison shrugged. "He seemed pretty cool." We were now walking out of one room and headed to the other. "I've gotten to know Ms. Vee over the last few weeks."

I clenched my jaw as the small hairs on the back of my neck stood to attention. "And your thoughts?"

"She's something else. If Mr. Reid named her as his successor, I wouldn't sweat it. I think that woman can do whatever the hell she puts her mind to." His smile grew. "And she's nice, you know? Like Grant Marsh can be an ass sometimes. Not Vee. She knows her stuff and isn't afraid to ask questions when she doesn't."

Dennison and I joined the rest of the team and settled into chairs in the large viewing room.

"Do you know her?" Dennison asked in a whisper.

"Maeve Hubbard?" I asked, playing dumb. When Dennison nodded, I nodded back. "Yeah, I do. I agree with your assessment. Anyone who doubts her capabilities doesn't know her."

"Gentlemen," Coach Tilson said. "We're going to

have an abbreviated viewing today. You kicked LA's ass."

All the players cheered. Everyone was supposed to be present, the fifty-three active players and the sixteen on the practice squad. As I looked around, I realized we were down from that number. Then I remembered Pratt telling us that Sean Lester, a defensive linebacker, was on the IR. He was probably with the medical staff this morning as well as a few other players. Football had a way of keeping the medical staff busy.

Less than an hour later, Coach Tilson stopped the video. "Lunch and then position meetings. If you need to visit the trainers, make your way there before or after position meetings. Then go home. Ms. Hubbard didn't tell you what to say if you're questioned by a reporter because let's face it—she's a hell of a lot nicer than I am."

"Prettier too," Simpson murmured to my side.

The players around him nodded encouragingly as I clenched my jaw.

"I'm telling you," Coach Tilson continued, "'no comment' is the only fucking comment that should be recorded by any one of you. If it's not... If I read a comment attributed to a Coopers player, I'm coming for you." The room was deadly quiet. "Reid Hubbard deserves more than our best play. He deserves our respect. That respect filters down to everyone in the executive offices. Vee called all of you family. Act like it.

Tonight and tomorrow are not times for you to be downtown at bars or clubs. Everything everyone in this room does during the next few days or week will be scrutinized. Don't give anyone anything to make into a headline." He paused but no one raised their hand. "Come back on Wednesday ready to work your asses off to prepare for the Raiders. They're at 4 and 1. Sunday won't be a walk in the park. Who's in?"

"We are, Coach," came from every player.

"Who's in?"

Even louder yet. "We are, Coach."

"See you Wednesday, ready to practice hard."

As we stood, I met Simpson's gaze. "She's more than pretty."

Simpson turned my direction. "I didn't mean anything by it."

With my lips pressed together, I stared into his eyes. "I just wanted to let you know there's more to her than looks."

Simpson leaned back and lifted his hands. "Again, no offense."

I stretched my fingers, resisting the desire to ball them into fists. The irresistible urge to shove this cocky kid against the wall was almost too much to fight. In my mind, I had Simpson pinned against the wall with my forearm to his neck. As his face grew a darker shade of crimson, I would explain exactly who Maeve Hubbard was.

She was intelligent and fun, kind and compassionate. Her smile lit up a room or an entire football field. Her loyalty and dedication were without bounds. She was stunningly beautiful whether she was waking up or dressed for a social event. Her purpose overtook her fears. She'd never met a challenge she couldn't conquer. Yet she could be confident and vulnerable at the same time.

I gritted my teeth. Vee wasn't as shallow as the word pretty.

Dennison's shoulder bumped into mine. "Let's go eat some lunch." After Simpson walked away, Dennison spoke softly. "Are you all right? What was that?"

"The woman just lost her father. She doesn't need stupid-ass comments about her looks."

"Yeah, all right. Maybe you need to go see that new woman of yours and work out these frustrations."

My smile returned. "I told you. I don't have frustrations."

"Sure."

During lunch, no one from the executive offices entered the cafeteria. I knew, because I kept an eagle eye on the entry. My every thought was about Vee. While I'd checked my phone between meetings, I didn't have any messages from her.

I managed to speak civilly with Simpson during the quarterback meeting. Once it was over, I didn't waste any time making small talk as I gathered my shit together and headed out to my truck.

Once I threw my bag in the back seat, I checked my phone for the hundredth time. My heart skipped a beat at the sight of Vee's name. The text message had arrived only a few minutes earlier.

"I'M STILL NOT DONE AT DAPHNE'S HOUSE. I'M NOT SURE WHEN I'LL BE HOME."

I TEXTED BACK.

"I DON'T WANT YOU TO BE ALONE TONIGHT."

HER REPLY CAME IMMEDIATELY.

"DOES THAT MEAN YOU'LL STAY OVER AGAIN?"

"IF YOU WANT ME, I'LL GO HOME AND GET MY THINGS AND HEAD BACK TO YOUR PLACE."

. . .

"I WANT YOU. I'LL TEXT WHEN THIS SHITTY FAMILY MEETING FINALLY ENDS."

I CONSIDERED my next text before hitting send.

"I LOVE YOU, VEE HUBBARD. (Heart emoji)

I HIT SEND.

Instead of the smooth exit from the parking lot, there was a line of traffic forming at the front gate to the complex. By the time I made it to the gate, I saw the reason for the delay. There were multiple news vans, many with local call letters, but there were others from national outlets: ESPN, FOX SPORTS, and PARA-MOUNT. Reporters stood near the road, screaming questions toward the vehicles leaving.

It appeared everyone was following Coach Tilson's orders. No one was stopping.

Thank God Vee said she was at Daphne's house. That meant she wasn't seeing this circus, at least not yet.

CHAPTER 6

Vee

The air in the sitting room of Dad and Daphne's home was tense, adding to my growing headache.

"It's not what Reid would want," Daphne said, wiping away tears. Her inhibitions were lost about four rum and Diet Cokes ago. "He deserves more."

Inhaling, I closed my eyes, opening them to Aunt Rachel's stare. The sight of my aunt gave me an idea. I turned my attention to Cammy Wilcox, the president of Coopers' legal division. Seated next to Cammy was Joseph Eads, Dad's personal attorney. To round out the legal advisors, my cousin Leigh was sitting at my side.

"Cammy," I asked, "this discussion has gone on too long. Who has the legal right to plan the funeral, the co-executors or Daphne?"

Daphne stood and spun toward me, her eyes trying to focus. "I'm right here, Vee." Her volume rose. "You want to ask me a question, ask me."

"Oh, I wasn't aware of your law degree. I'm asking for legal advice."

Leigh covered my hand with hers as Grant directed Daphne back to her seat.

Cammy was the one to speak. "The executors are primarily in charge of finances. The funeral planning, if not designated in the will, which it seems it wasn't, is left up to family."

"Spouse and child," Leigh said.

"Spouse and then adult children," Cammy explained. "I'm sorry, Vee."

"Doesn't the list go on?" I asked.

Cammy nodded. "Spouse, adult children, parents, and siblings."

"Aunt Rachel," I began, "in that listing, you too have a vote. Do you think Dad would want a grand spectacle around his funeral?"

"No."

Everyone in the room turned to Daphne. "It's my decision. That's what Cammy just said. I won't allow a man like Reid to simply fade away."

"He won't," I said, arguing my case. "We, family and close friends, will have a private funeral and celebration of life. At the next home game, we'll have a moment of silence. At the end of the season, we can have a special commemoration and have Dad's name permanently placed on a banner at Crystal Light Stadium. It's all very simple and yet respectful, just like Dad." I turned to Daphne. "Dad wasn't into spectacles." My jaw clenched, keeping the rest of my statement from coming out—unlike you.

We all watched—Uncle Darin, Aunt Rachel, Grant, Lip, Leigh, me, and the attorneys—as Daphne pressed her lips together and pushed off with her high heels, twisting her chair one way and the other.

"Private?" Daphne asked. "How private?"

"Invitation only," I replied. "We don't need thousands of fans coming to get a last look at Reid Hubbard."

Aunt Rachel was sitting near Daphne. "I have to agree," she said. "This is a time for family and close friends."

New tears came to my stepmother's eyes. "I don't understand why Reid didn't have this all planned." She turned to Mr. Eads. "Why wasn't this discussed?"

Joseph Eads pressed his lips together and shrugged. "I tried. Reid wasn't ready to face his mortality. He was still healthy and young." He looked around the room. "I brought up the outdated will many times."

Uncle Darin stood. "He was talking to us about it. He planned on signing a new one after the end of the season."

"How old is Dad's will?" I asked.

"Twenty-three years," Mr. Eads proclaimed. "That is Reid's last will and testament." He nodded toward Cammy Wilcox. "The Coopers' succession had been updated more recently."

"When?" I asked.

"Within the last ten years," Ms. Wilcox said. "We have time to further discuss all of this after the final arrangements are made." She nodded toward Daphne. "Mrs. Hubbard, are we all in agreement of a private funeral and celebration of life, a moment of silence and a commemoration of life at the end of the season?"

"Football," Daphne murmured. "His entire life was monopolized by football. I suppose it makes sense that his death would be too."

I took that as my cue. Standing, I turned to Ms. Wilcox. "Thank you, Cammy. Once we have the particulars, we'll inform you and..." I looked at Grant. "The Coopers will communicate to our fans." I lifted my satchel. "Daphne, we can talk tomorrow. I think we're all too exhausted tonight."

She pursed her lips and nodded with a huff.

I spoke to the room. "Nothing is finalized until Daphne and I have a chance to voice our opinions."

My stepmother's brown stare came my way. "Thank you for including me."

"I have a headache. Good night, everyone."

"Vee," Leigh called out. "Do you need a ride home?"

"Thanks. I think I need some time alone."

My cousin got up and followed me to the door. "Will you be?" she asked quietly.

"Alone?"

Leigh nodded.

"No." I exhaled. "I won't."

"Good." She wrapped her arms around me. "Let me know when you're home."

"Vee," Mr. Eads said, "may I accompany you out to your car?"

"I'm tired."

"This is important, I promise."

Nodding, I opened the front door.

Dad and Daphne's home was located on twenty-five acres northeast of the city. Stepping outside, I inhaled the humid autumn air. The earlier rain was gone, leaving its remnants in the form of puddles and saturated air. A cloud deck hovered over the western horizon, displaying an array of colors—reds, oranges, and purples.

"Vee," Mr. Eads said, closing the door to the rest of the family. "Again, I'm sorry for your loss."

"Mr. Eads, what couldn't wait another day?"

"Did your father ever discuss his will with you?"

I inhaled. "Recently, he told me he was considering changes, including Uncle Darin, Aunt Rachel, Grant,

Lip, and Leigh for thirty-nine percent. He said I'd have fifty-one percent, controlling interest."

Mr. Eads nodded. "That was what was discussed. I even drafted a new will."

"Did Dad sign the draft?"

He shook his head. "Your father constructed his will around the time he and Daphne married. I was with your father at that time. After your mother, Reid was cautious."

"Did Dad and Daphne have a prenup?"

"No. That was why he didn't want to leave his vast estate or the Coopers' future to chance. In his will he provided for his children, in the case he and Daphne would have more. As you know, you're his only child. Nevertheless, time changed things, and he was willing to broaden the beneficiaries."

"But he didn't...not yet?"

"No, he didn't."

"Mr. Eads," I asked, "what are you trying to tell me?"

"I'm letting you know, Vee, that when the dust settles, it will be clear to everyone that Reid left everything to you."

I opened my eyes wider. "Everything?" Lifting my chin, I looked over the brick driveway, the fountain, and the expansive manicured lawn. "The house and property?"

Mr. Eads nodded. "Again, after your mother, he was

skeptical. Recently, he realized that Daphne wasn't Olivia. He wanted Daphne to be taken care of and the Marshes to have a stake in the Coopers."

"What are you suggesting is done?"

"I think you should consider honoring his wishes. I'll be happy to show you the drafted will."

"The one Dad didn't sign?"

"Well, yes."

"Mr. Eads, first, I'll put my father to rest. Next, I will do whatever is possible to keep the Coopers the successful franchise my father led. Dealing with his vast estate and desires will have to wait."

"Daphne?"

"She won't be evicted. I have no desire to live in this house ever again."

"As your property, you will be responsible for taxes and maintenance."

"I'm going to say this in a way that I hope you understand. My father is dead. I do not wish to deal with any of these matters in the immediate future. If you are unable to represent me and my best interests, I'll seek my own counsel."

"Vee, I've known you since you were a child. Of course I want what's best for you. I also want what your father would want."

"If Dad truly wanted his will changed after over twenty years, he would have done it. Good night." I turned and walked to my car, my heels clipping the brick pavers.

Slamming my car door, I pushed the ignition button. The interior filled with music as I looked down at my phone. My temples throbbed at the long list of missed calls and text messages—Emma from college. I rolled my eyes at Preston's name. Unwilling to tackle the feat, I tossed my phone into my bag.

My car contained a transponder to open and close the gate at the end of the long driveway. As I approached, I saw the crowd gathered outside the gate. A Fayette County Sheriff's car was stationed outside. As the gate began to open, a deputy stepped onto the property.

I lowered the music and rolled down my window.

"Ma'am," the deputy said, stepping closer.

"Thank you for being here. Do we need to contract private security?"

"Our orders are to watch Mr. Hubbard's home until after the funeral."

"Thank you," I said again. "Do you know if the stadium, football center, or my condominium are being watched?"

The crowd beyond the gate was yelling questions.

"Those properties are within Lexington proper. They would be monitored by the Lexington Police Department."

"I'll find out," I said. "Thank you. More people will be leaving shortly."

He tipped his hat. "Sorry for your loss, ma'am."

Nodding, I closed my window. The deputy stepped outside the gate, pushing the people away, and giving me a clear road to escape. I quickly called Uncle Darin and asked him to warn the others about the crowd of reporters.

About ten minutes from home, my phone rang. Fin's name was on the dashboard screen. Hitting the green icon, I spoke, "I'm almost home."

"Vee, I think you should come to my place."

"I want to be home."

"I'm at the Vine. You don't want to be here. I can't fathom a way of getting you from the garage to your condo. As you know, the first floor is public and right now, every reporter present wants to get an exclusive from you."

"Shit." Tears prickled the back of my eyes.

"I'm sorry."

It shouldn't hit me as hard as it did, yet the air seemed to vanish from my lungs, and my hands began to tremble. "I just want..." There were so many things I wanted. "You're there?"

"I'm in my car now."

"If I can't go home, I need things. I can't show up tomorrow in the same clothes. I'll call the concierge and get you a keycard that opens my apartment. Call when you're outside and I'll give you the security code. Please bring me clothes for tonight and tomorrow. Throw cosmetics into a bag, there's one under the bathroom sink. I'll make whatever you bring work."

"I'll do it."

"Oh, and Fin?"

"Yes?"

"Send me your address."

CHAPTER 7

Fin

Donning an old Cincinnati Reds baseball cap, I pulled the bill down over my eyes and made my way through the crowded first level of the Vine. The same kid who had been on duty at the concierge desk the night I was given a reusable keycard was standing behind the desk. The phone receiver was to his ear, and a solemn expression was on his face.

"He's here, Ms. Hubbard. I have an idea if you don't mind?"

I couldn't hear Vee's answer, but I took a step closer.

"I have a keycard," he began, "that can get you from the garage to the seventh floor with no stops. It's a bypass card usually used for medical emergencies. If you'd like..." His lips curled into a smile. "Yes, here he is." The kid handed me the receiver.

"Fin?" Vee's voice came through.

"I'm here. I'll do whatever you want."

"I want to be home, and I want you to be with me."

I nodded and read the kid's name tag. "Ethan and I will do whatever it takes."

"Thank you. I should be home in less than ten minutes. My security code for my condo is 0-4-2-6-1-1." Before I could ask why she told me the code, she said, "Please give the phone back to Ethan."

"I'll see you soon." I handed the receiver back to Ethan. "She wants to talk to you."

"Ms. Hubbard?" he said. The rest of their conversation consisted of nods and the affirmative adverb—yes, I can do that.

Once he hung up the phone, Ethan asked me to wait. He again slid a keycard into the machine and pressed a few keys on the keyboard. When the key popped out, he handed it to me. "This replaces your other keycard and allows you entry into 706."

That was why she shared the security code. A smile came to my lips. "Ms. Hubbard requested this?"

"Yes, sir, she did."

Keeping my eyes down, I made my way through the people. Back outside, I reparked my truck in a long-term parking space, retrieved my duffel bag and a sack of groceries from the back seat. Again, I forged my way through the crowd to the elevator.

"Fin."

I heard my name as I entered the elevator. While I didn't answer, I lifted my chin in time to see someone take my picture. Gritting my teeth, I chose to continue my quest. I had just enough time to take my things up to Vee's place and get back down to Ethan.

Thankfully, recalling numbers wasn't a problem. After opening her door, I entered Vee's security code.

With two minutes to spare, I made my way back to Ethan. Together, we took the back stairs to the garage.

My breath caught as Vee's white Mercedes-Benz pulled into the garage and into her assigned parking space. I didn't wait for her to get out. Instead, I hurried to the driver's door. Vee's swollen, tear-filled eyes looked up through the window, causing my chest to ache. As soon as she opened the door, I offered her my hand.

Hers trembled as it landed in my grasp.

"Let's get you upstairs."

Vee nodded, reached for her leather bag, stood, and leaned against my chest. As she buried her face against my shirt, I led her toward the elevator.

"Wait there," Ethan said. "I want to make sure there's no one getting off."

The doors opened to an empty compartment.

"We're good to go," he said, holding the doors. "I'm so sorry for your loss, Ms. Hubbard."

"Thank you for helping me." Despite her exhausted appearance, her words sounded strong.

We remained quiet as the doors closed and Ethan used his magic card. The elevator bypassed other floors, going straight up to the seventh floor. The doors opened with a ding.

"If you want a similar ride in the morning, please give us a call. I don't get on duty until noon, but Jacob can help you earlier."

"Thank you, Ethan," I said.

He held the doors open as Vee and I exited. The seventh-floor hallway was clear of people as we made our way to her door. The new keycard I'd been given worked for the second time. Once again, I disarmed the security and locked the door behind us.

"Thank you," Vee said, wrapping her arms around my midsection. Her words were muffled by her face pressed against my chest.

For a moment, I simply stroked her hair and gently caressed a circle on her back. In my arms, Vee's body trembled. Sobs that I wanted to take away bubbled from her throat and tears dampened my shirt.

"Tell me what to do," I pleaded, wanting nothing more than to make her world right.

"You're doing it." She looked up, meeting my gaze.

"All day, I didn't cry. I mean, I did, but I couldn't let go. I had to stay strong."

My lips kissed the top of her head. "You don't have to be strong with me." I led her through the condo to the sofa and pulled her down to my lap. The ache in my heart and the need to comfort Vee had been building throughout the day. Now that she was here in my arms, I longed to make the world right if only for a few minutes.

"One of the reasons I fell in love with you all those years ago," I said, "was because I didn't have to pretend when I was with you." I stroked her cheek. "You don't have to pretend, Vee. I know you're strong. I can't imagine what you've been through today or what the future holds. I just know that I love you for showing me the Maeve Hubbard the rest of the world doesn't get to see."

She scoffed, wiping her eye and smearing her mascara. "Not exactly a pretty picture."

I palmed her cheeks. "You're real and real is the most beautiful picture."

Vee laid her cheek against my shoulder.

"I'll stand to your side and admire you, lie with you and make love to you, hold your hand to let you know you're not alone, or carry you when you're not ready to walk. Whatever you need."

Her body convulsed with hiccups as she looked up and forced a smile. "I'm thankful you're here."

"I'm sorry this happened."

She nodded. "It was an accident. A stupid accident. From what we were told, a semi-truck changed lanes too fast, didn't see Dad's car..." She returned her forehead to my shoulder. "I saw him—Dad."

I splayed my fingers over the warm skin of her lower back. "I would have gone with you."

She shook her head. "I needed to do it. Uncle Darin was there." Vee looked back up, meeting my gaze. "If you'd been there, I wouldn't have stayed strong. Reid Hubbard didn't raise me to fall apart."

"I would assume he raised you to be true to your feelings. You can do both."

Her nose wrinkled as she sat up. "I want to shower."

"Do you want help?"

Vee shook her head. "Sounds tempting, but I think I want to get my tears out and wash away the stench of the morgue."

"What have you eaten today?"

"The eggs and vegetables you made this morning."

"I'll cook us dinner while you shower."

Her cheeks rose, and her green eyes seemed to clear. "I don't remember you being so domestic."

I shrugged. "Living alone for most of my life can do that. My mom taught me how to cook and not starve. I stopped by the store and picked up steaks, potatoes, and salad."

"I don't eat meat."

I made the connection. "Oh, that's why you didn't have bacon."

"You're right."

"Okay, I'll figure something out."

"You can eat whatever you want," Vee said. "My choice to stop eating meat was more about health than any high moral ground." She stood.

I maintained my grasp of her hand and stood. "Did you tell him goodbye?"

More tears flooded her eyes. "I told him I loved him. I can't remember the particulars." She freed her hand and wiped her nose on her arm. "They're doing an autopsy before sending him to the funeral home."

"Why?"

"Some stupid state requirement for fatal accidents."

"When should it be done?"

Vee turned toward the large clock over her fire-place. "I don't know. The man at the coroner's office said usually twenty-four to forty-eight hours. They'll probably notify Daphne when it's done. I couldn't stay at her house another minute. I wanted to scream."

I smiled. "You can do that too if you want."

"I did in the car."

"Shower and get comfortable." I brushed my lips over hers.

Vee took a few steps and stopped, turning back to me. "How many reporters were downstairs?"

"I don't know for sure. The first floor was more crowded than on a game-day Sunday."

"There were reporters camped outside Dad's property."

"I guess that's Daphne's property now."

Vee shook her head. "I'll tell you about that after my shower."

Watching her walk toward her bedroom, I recalled what I'd wanted to say to Simpson. Maeve was more than pretty. She was intelligent and fun, kind and compassionate. Her smile lit up a room or an entire football field. Her loyalty and dedication were without bounds. She was stunningly beautiful whether she was waking up or dressed for a social event. Her purpose overtook her fears. She'd never met a challenge she couldn't conquer. Yet she could be confident and vulnerable at the same time.

"Vee," I called.

"Hmm?" She turned my way.

"Whatever the future holds, you will not only survive but conquer."

CHAPTER 8

Vee

"I want to stay here like this forever," I said, lying on the floor, covered by a blanket. I was positioned between Fin's long legs, my head resting on his chest, and a roaring fire in front of us. After my shower, I'd chosen soft pajama pants and a sweatshirt. My stomach was filled with the delicious salad Fin assembled using the kit he'd bought and adding a variety of items such as vegetables, tofu, and almonds. He too had a salad, but his included slices of medium-rare fillet.

We each had our second glass of wine on the nearby coffee table. However, my gaze was set on the flames, reminding me of the sky earlier in the evening.

"Don't think about what comes next," Fin said. "Let yourself rest."

His words vibrated his chest and resonated through the condominium.

"I'm sorry," I said.

"What do you have to be sorry about?"

"I wanted you to get to know Dad. I was ready to tell him about us this morning. If only I'd asked to meet him—"

Fin hugged me tighter. "Don't do that, Vee. Nothing about what happened could have been prevented with the words...*if only*."

Pressing my lips together, I craned my neck and peered upward. "There are some things I haven't told you."

"Do you want to tell me?"

I nodded as my focus went back to the flames. "I need to think about them and talking would help. The only other person I could talk to about these things is Leigh, and while I trust her, I'm not sure about her parents—Aunt Rachel, I am. It's Uncle Darin..." I shook my head. "I'm rambling."

Fin leaned forward and kissed the top of my head. "Talking is good. As for your family, I don't truly understand the dynamics. From what I recall, your mom left when you were young."

"Very." I exhaled. "Not my favorite subject. However, for what's happening, my mother is irrelevant. Dad did the best he could. When I was very young, there were nannies, but from the time I was school-age, it was mostly Dad and me. Aunt Rachel was close. She tried to fill in where she could." My cheeks lifted with a weak smile. "Honestly, Dad didn't leave many gaps. He never made me feel like I was second. Until Daphne."

Fin caressed my arms. "Spend your time with the memories of your good relationship."

The guilt returned. "I wish I had told him about you."

"What about your uncle and cousins? Did I sense some issues during my contract renegotiation meeting?"

Issues.

"Royce Beasley, general manager and no relation, has never thought of me as a significant part of the Coopers. Uncle Darin and Grant fall under that category too. Being the oldest grandchild of Grandpa Carroll, Grant feels he's entitled to the team." I sat up and turned toward Fin. "Grandpa Carroll left the entirety of the franchise to Dad, even though he divided his estate with Dad's sister, Aunt Rachel."

Small lines appeared near Fin's blue eyes. "Why did he cut her out of the franchise?"

"I don't know," I answered honestly. "I asked her this morning."

"This morning?"

"I know. Bad timing. I hadn't given it a lot of thought until now."

"Because you're worried your dad would cut you out?"

I shook my head. "I found out tonight as I was leaving Daphne's that Dad's last will is over twenty years old. Outdated, according to Dad's personal attorney, Joseph Eads. According to Mr. Eads and Uncle Darin, Dad was on the verge of changing his will. He and I talked about it. He said it could wait until after the season."

Fin's forehead furrowed. "I don't understand. Is the old will bad?"

It was hard for me to form the words, the ones that I'd been thinking about since I left Daphne's house—or where she lived. "The old will leaves everything, the estate and one hundred percent of the franchise, to me."

Fin's eyes opened wide. "And the will is how old?"

"Over twenty years."

"Your dad left everything to you when you were only fourteen years old?"

I shrugged. "Cammy, the Coopers' head of legal, said a more recent change had happened with the team, but as for his estate, yeah. Mr. Eads said when the will was written, Dad was still burnt by my mother. He was about to marry or had just married Daphne. They didn't have a prenup." Another shrug. "I didn't know anything about that stuff at the time. Anyway, Dad wanted to be sure the Coopers stayed within the family. He also didn't want Daphne to try to take my inheritance."

"Fuck, Vee, you're—"

"Screwed? Over my head? Overwhelmed? Pick one or come up with something better."

Fin reached for my hands. "You're the sole heir to billions."

"I don't know about billions."

"I do. I researched different teams before deciding on the Coopers." He reached for his phone from the table.

As he did, I seized the stem of my wine glass and took a hearty drink.

"Here," he said, reading his phone. "Your grandfather purchased the Coopers for twenty million dollars in 1978. Today, the Coopers and, according to this website, your father, have an estimated worth of six billion dollars."

I closed my eyes and groaned.

"I'm not saying that a random internet search is the best way to determine the value of your father's estate, but I would presume it's relatively close."

Opening my eyes, I searched Fin's stare. "Does this make you want to stop whatever we have going on? Or does this make you...I don't know, only want me for the money?"

His laugh filled the air. "Neither."

"Neither?"

Fin leaned forward and took hold of my hands. "I'm not a billionaire, but money will never be an issue for me. So for the record, I'm not looking for a sugar mama. And as for running, I did that once. The reason was the opposite of what's happening now."

"I'm talking to you?" I tilted my head.

"Yes, Vee. We're talking. My offers from before stand. I will be next to you, behind you, or holding your hand. It's not like you just won the lottery."

I shook my head, remembering Dad on that table.

"It is more like you inherited a lot."

"A lot," I repeated.

His eyes narrowed. "What was your dad going to change in the new will?"

"According to him, he was going to give me fifty-one percent of the Coopers."

"Controlling interest."

I nodded. "Thirty-nine percent would go to Uncle Darin and Aunt Rachel to be later divided between Grant, Philip, and Leigh."

"That's only ninety percent," Fin said.

"I said the same thing to Dad. He said Daphne wanted a percentage."

"And none of that is in writing?"

Pressing my lips together, I sighed. "Mr. Eads said he drafted the changed will. Dad never signed it."

"What is Mr. Eads suggesting?"

"He's suggesting I agree to split the Coopers the way Dad had intended."

"And his estate?"

"I honestly don't know. I would assume Daphne would get the house and land."

"Who knows about the wills?" Fin asked.

"The attorneys, Uncle Darin, Aunt Rachel...well, I'm not sure what Daphne knows, but the rest of the family is well informed. Uncle Darin isn't happy."

"How do you feel?"

"Talking to Joseph Eads made me think I should get my own representation."

"You don't think he's looking out for your best interests?"

"I don't know, Fin. I wish I didn't have to think about any of this until after Dad's funeral."

"Why do you have to?"

Sighing, I stood and slapped my palms against my thighs. "My family is...they can be intense. It took hours for us to agree on the funeral plans. Getting agreement on billions in assets will be impossible."

Fin stood, meeting me chest to chest. "Vee, agreement isn't necessary. As of sometime this morning, you are the sole beneficiary of Reid Hubbard's last will and testament and the sole owner of the Coopers."

My eyes opened wide. "What about us? Does the change affect your contract?"

"I don't think so. I can have Jackson investigate it in the morning."

I shook my head. "Please don't. I don't want Jackson knowing more than my family." I tilted my head. "How were your meetings?"

"Somber. Tilson told us all to go home and mourn. Then to come back on Wednesday ready to beat the Raiders."

Taking a step closer, I wrapped my arms around Fin's toned torso. "I'm going to miss the time I spent with the players."

"Why? Keep doing it. You're in charge."

"I have a lot to learn about being in charge. I always assumed I had another ten to fifteen years for on-the-job training with Dad."

Fin reached for my chin and lifted it. After a soft kiss, he smiled. "Maeve Hubbard, you will succeed at whatever you set out to do. The players and coaches are one hundred percent behind you. The staff at Maker's Mark and Crystal Light love and respect you. It seems to me that the only resistance you're worried about is from within the executive offices."

"There's a lot to be concerned about. I may have learned a little about play calling, but there is so much more I don't know."

"Who does?"

"Everyone...my family. We all have our strengths. Together we're stronger."

Fin inhaled, his chest pressing against my breasts. "Then keep everyone together. They have worked with your father without owning interest in the Coopers. If you choose to honor his original will, you aren't changing anything."

"Other than it's me at the top."

Fin's lips quirked. "You're amazing on top." He tugged at my hand. "Come on. I don't have to go into Maker's Mark tomorrow, but I bet you do."

"I do."

"I'm going with you."

"I could argue."

"You could," he agreed. "I plan on winning."

"That's why you were the right pick for our team." I lifted my phone and wine glass from the table. After finishing the wine, I entered the passcode on my phone. My momentary smile faded. "Oh shit. I turned off the volume."

"Did you miss any messages?"

Scrolling, I saw that I'd missed many. There was a missed call from Preston, but that wasn't what garnered my attention. "Two calls from Uncle Darin. He left a text message." I looked at the time stamp. "Shit, this was over two hours ago." I read the message. "Autopsy results are in. Answer your phone."

I looked up at Fin. "It hasn't been twenty-four hours."

Fin shrugged. "I'm not sure how it works. Maybe they fast-tracked it?"

"It's after ten. Should I call?"

"If you don't, will you be able to sleep?"

I shook my head and hit the call button.

CHAPTER 9

Fin

"I just saw the message. Well, I'm calling now," Vee said, her volume increasing. "I didn't think they'd have answers this soon." She pressed her lips together. "Tell me about the autopsy results." Biting her lip, she nodded. "Wait. I want to write this down."

I followed Vee to her office near the entry to her condo. After flipping on the light, she went to her desk, laid the phone on the glass surface, and hit the speaker button.

"I'm ready." Her green stare came to me, and she motioned for me to stay.

The voice coming from her phone was Darin Marsh, Vee's uncle. "The police emphasized that these results are preliminary."

The muscles on the side of her face pulled tight as she looked up at me. "What did they find?"

"Preliminary cause of death was basilar skull fracture. They believe in the impact with the truck, his neck snapped forward and back. The injury was so severe it was instantly fatal. The basilar is a bone at the base of the skull."

Vee wrote the words and swallowed. She underlined the word instantly.

Darin continued, "They did an external and internal inspection, examined Reid's organs, and collected samples for toxicology. So far, they've gotten the initial test results. They were looking for the presence or absence of general drug classes. He warned that these early tests may have false positives."

"Did they find anything?"

"Reid's blood alcohol level was only trace, below the legal limit."

"He had drinks at the game," Vee said.

"And Daphne said he had a whiskey before bed."

"Anything else?"

"Benzodiazepines, beta blockers, and antihistamines were also found. They haven't yet determined the amount."

"Was Dad taking those?"

"Daphne only said he took a beta blocker for high blood pressure. She didn't mention the other two medications," Darin replied.

"Are they releasing his body?"

"It's already been transported to the mortuary. Now you and Daphne need to decide on the schedule for services."

Vee stopped writing. "Thanks, Uncle Darin. I'll be in touch with Daphne in the morning."

"Vee?" Darin hesitated. "Did Joe Eads talk to you about the will he drafted?"

Vee's neck straightened and her shoulders went back. "We'll bury my father before we discuss that. As for the Coopers, everyone needs to do their job—what we've been doing. It's the only way we'll make it through this. Good night." She didn't wait for his response. After hitting the red icon, she pushed her phone away and looked up at me. "You heard."

I had. It was a conversation that no one wanted to have. There was one bit of good news. I tried to capitalize on that. "Instant is what we all wish for."

Her green eyes flooded with new tears. "I wish Dad was still with us, but if he has to be gone, instant is better than thinking about him suffering."

I offered Vee my hand. "Let's try to get some sleep."

Nodding, she laid her palm in mine and stood.

After getting ready for bed, I offered Vee my shoulder for a pillow. Without hesitation, she curled her warm petite body next to mine. As we lay in the darkness, my mind went back to a time when we were both at the University of Kentucky.

The reason I didn't call Vee after I left U of K now seemed to be more of a blessing than a curse. The woman at my side was still *my* Vee, the beautiful girl I saved from a group of drunk football players. She was still the woman who accepted me without expecting perfection. Not knowing about her father back then allowed me to fall in love with her, not her family's notoriety.

I wasn't certain how much time passed before Vee's breathing took on a soft rhythm of its own and her head seemed heavier. Craning my neck, I kissed the top of her hair and whispered, "I'm not going to leave you again."

Tuesday morning, I woke up to the sound of water spraying in the shower. Instead of joining Vee, I went to the kitchen and started the coffee maker. A search of her refrigerator had me making a mental shopping list. While she was probably fine surviving on rabbit food, there was now a professional quarterback taking up residence, albeit temporarily, who needed more calories than was found in oatmeal and tofu.

As soon as the coffee finished brewing, I took a cup with cream into the bathroom. Placing it on the vanity, I scanned her long, wet hair, down her towel-covered body, and sexy legs. I brushed Vee's cheek with a kiss.

She feigned a smile. "I think it's a first, or at least a first since we decided to get back together."

"What's a first?"

"We spent the night together without having sex."

My cheeks rose. "Oh, I thought about it."

Laying her hand on my bare shoulder, she leaned closer. "I did too, but I think I needed what you gave me—a shoulder to cry on and the comfort of not being alone."

"Do you mind if I shower? While you..." I shrugged. "Do whatever it is you do?"

"I don't mind. But if you drop those shorts and there's nothing underneath them, I may have to reevaluate what I need to do."

I stood behind her, peering over her in the mirror and wrapping my arms around her waist. Lowering my voice, I deepened my tone. "Ms. Hubbard, whenever you need my cock buried in your tight pussy, I'm available." I wiggled my eyebrows in the reflection. "As we speak, I'm getting hard."

Pink filled her cheeks as she wiggled her sexy ass against my growing erection.

"If you want to start your day with a quick fuck, I'm not opposed."

Pressing her lips together, Vee shook her head. "I do want that and I'll take comfort in knowing it was offered." She sighed. "It's nice to spend even a few minutes thinking about something good."

"Well, fuck. I guess that means my shower will be cold."

"Poor Fin," Vee scoffed.

I made eye contact in the mirror as I dropped trou, my erection standing to attention. "You did this."

"Guilty as charged." She turned, facing me and leaning against the vanity. Her focus was not on my eyes as she nibbled her bottom lip. "I'll take a raincheck."

The cold shower did little to lessen the rigidity of my cock. If I were alone, I could have managed the issue, but I didn't think masturbating was the best use of my time. The thoughts of what Vee had in store for the day and for her future helped tame my penis into submission.

Stepping out of the shower, I wrapped a towel around my waist. "What are your plans for today?"

"I think I'll go first to Maker's Mark. I want to meet with people first and get everyone's mind set on the Raiders game. Then when I'm done there, I'll head over to Daphne's. She and I need to finalize the arrangements for the funeral."

"I'll go with you."

"How about you don't?"

My head tilted as I took her in. "I told you last night, I'd argue about this and win."

Vee nodded. "You said Tilson told everyone to stay home today. If you're at the football center, there will be questions."

"You were ready to tell your dad."

"I was." She inhaled. "Now I can't. Please don't

think this means I don't want what's happening. It just means my plate is overflowing at the moment."

"Okay," I said, nodding. "Speaking of plates, I'll make some breakfast."

Wearing blue jeans and a Coopers t-shirt, I slid the spatula beneath the omelet, I flipped it as Vee emerged from the bedroom. My lips curled as I took her in, from her pulled-back hair, bright emerald eyes, and down her satin top and navy skirt to her matching shoes. "You're stunning as always."

She came closer. "I could get used to all this cooking. As long as you're okay with me gaining forty pounds."

"You could stand to gain some weight. Forty..." I shrugged. "I'd still love you."

Vee hummed as she looked down in the pan.

"Vegetable omelet with Swiss cheese."

"In the other pan?" she asked.

"Vegetable and bacon omelet with Swiss cheese. Grab some plates."

Soon, we were both seated at the large kitchen island, eating and sipping our coffee. I'd been thinking about her request to handle today without me. "I get that you need to do today alone. What about tonight?"

She lowered her fork. "I'm being selfish."

"You want to be alone?"

"No," she answered quickly. "I'm selfish because I don't want to be alone. I also want to be here."

"You haven't seen my place. You might love downsizing."

"Fin, will you please plan on staying here" —she shrugged— "for a while." She started talking faster. "I'm not asking you to move in. I'm just asking…well, if you don't want to—"

My kiss interrupted her.

"You're rambling again."

Her lips curled. "Your answer?"

"After I get you safely down to your car, I'll go to my place and pack more clothes and clean out my refrigerator. Yours is woefully sparse."

"Thank you."

Vee's phone vibrated on the marble surface. The name Grant was on her screen. She rolled her eyes and picked up the phone. "Grant, what couldn't wait for me to get to Maker's Mark?"

Her cousin's voice was loud enough for me to hear every word. "What the fuck is going on with you and Griffin Graham?"

CHAPTER 10

Vee

Pulling the phone from my ear, I looked at Fin, whose blue eyes were as round as saucers. While Grant's volume didn't require a speaker, I figured Fin should hear whatever my cousin was ranting about. I hit the speaker icon and laid the phone on the breakfast bar.

"Don't lie to me, Vee," Grant said. "Fin was in your building last evening."

"The Vine is a public building."

"Fucking Christ, you don't think we have enough going on? Have you seen the *Lexington Herald*? They ran the story online late last night. It's in today's paper, and it's been picked up all over the country."

"What are you talking about?"

"There's a picture of Fin going up the elevator in

your building, which for the record isn't public if you go higher than the first floor. The picture and accompanying story have had over a million views on social media. Outlets are running it beside the story about Uncle Reid."

"I haven't seen anything," I replied honestly.

Fin pushed his phone in front of me. My stomach dropped. There Fin was on the screen, wearing his old Cincinnati Reds ball cap. The caption below read:

Coopers' *starting quarterback helps football heiress grieve or is there more? Griffin Graham was seen carrying an overnight bag and groceries up a private elevator that leads to Maeve Hubbard's million-dollar condominium. Is our favorite football sideline heiress getting extracurricular with her players? What is happening now that Daddy is dead?*

Grant was still ranting as the omelet and coffee churned in my stomach. "Fin came by my place to help me bypass the reporters," I said. "This isn't news. It's tabloid gossip."

"I'm in charge of communications. How the hell am I supposed to spin this?"

"Don't."

"Don't?"

"It's sensationalism. We haven't spoken to the press

so they're digging for a story where there isn't one. Stick to our plan. I'll be at the football center soon. I'm calling an executive meeting for ten this morning."

"You're rushing things with this takeover."

"It's not a takeover. The Coopers weren't stolen nor was there a coup; they were thrust in my lap. I'm not going to let our tragedy take away from the season we started. Dad wanted a Super Bowl ring. I do too. I'll see you at ten o'clock." I hit the red icon and turned to Fin. "Shit. Just shit."

"Now I remember someone calling my name. I looked up. I was wearing the fucking hat to keep a low profile."

Inhaling, I stepped down from the stool and laid my hand on Fin's thigh. "I don't care about Grant or the story. People will believe what they want to believe. I'm not going to let this sidetrack—"

Fin's phone vibrated with an incoming call. The name Jackson was on the screen.

"Your agent?"

He nodded. "He must have seen the sensational story."

"I guess you could ask him if anything has changed now that..." There were too many ways to finish the sentence. "...things have changed."

"Hey," Fin said into his phone. "I just saw it."

Kissing his cheek, I walked back toward the bedroom. I needed to brush my teeth and head over to

Maker's Mark. Fin was still on the phone with Jackson Blanch when I started to leave. As I reached for my keys, I remembered the reporters from last night. One of them took Fin's picture.

I called down to the concierge's desk. Jacob answered on the second ring. As soon as I told him my name, he offered to meet me on the seventh floor and get me straight to the garage. "I'm sorry to be a bother."

"No bother, Ms. Hubbard."

I disconnected our call as Fin disconnected his. "How did that conversation go?"

"A little different than yours. Jackson already knew about us."

"What did he say about your contract?"

"He said he'd never had this situation before."

I smiled, my lips curling. "Yeah, it's a first for me too."

"Me too," Fin said as he came toward me. "Jackson said he'd investigate my contract, but due to the unlikelihood of such a situation, it probably isn't addressed in the fine print." His hands came to my hips, tugging me closer. "For the record, I'd give up playing before I gave you up."

"Don't say that. For one thing, the Coopers need you. For another, football has been your life. I don't want anyone to give anything up."

Fin kissed my nose before bringing his lips to mine.

My circulation warmed as his lips bruised mine.

Lifting my hands to his shoulders, I turned my head. We were performing a choreographed dance. It wasn't a continuation of what we once had. This was more. It was new with no walls between us. Despite my new title, I wasn't the one leading our dance. Fin's tongue teased my lips and willingly, I granted his entrance. Coffee mixed with my fresh mint breath as I lifted my fingers to his dark hair, weaving my fingers through his uncombed locks. By the time we pulled away from one another, my core was twisted and my nipples were hard.

Fin brought his nose to mine. "If you start to get sad or upset today, think about that kiss. Tonight won't be our second no-sex night."

"It won't?" I asked with a grin.

He shook his head.

Pushing up on my tiptoes, I kissed him softly. "I'll see you later. Jacob is probably waiting for me."

"Let me slip on some shoes. I'll go down with you and avoid the first floor. We don't want my picture in the paper—the morning-after walk of shame."

"Hurry up." I shrieked as Fin's hand landed on my ass with a slap. "Hey."

His blue eyes shone and his grin quirked. "You're getting a little too bossy. I thought I'd remind you who's in charge."

With my behind tingling, I met his gaze. "Yeah, maybe. I think I currently own you."

"My contract." He took long strides as he headed toward the bedroom.

I peeked outside the door as Jacob was coming down the hallway. "I'm sorry. We're almost ready."

"No problem, Ms. Hubbard."

"Are there many reporters downstairs?" I asked.

"There are more people than usual, but I don't know if they're reporters."

"Let's go," Fin said as he came toward us. Offering his hand, he approached Jacob. "I'm Griffin Graham; thank you for your help, Jacob."

Jacob's eyes opened wide. "You're Fin Graham."

"I am."

"It's nice to meet you."

"I'm certain," I said, "you'll keep our information confidential."

"Yes, Ms. Hubbard." He shook his head. "I'm sorry. I wasn't expecting..." He turned toward the open door. "I'll take you to the elevator."

Fin grinned as he laid his hand in the small of my back. "He must not have an X account."

"That makes one person."

CHAPTER 11

Vee

There were reporters outside the football center's front gate as I passed. Once again, a county sheriff's car was present, directing traffic and allowing employees of the Coopers to enter.

"Vee," Jen, my assistant, said as she saw me enter my front office, "you shouldn't be here today."

I feigned a smile. "I should. It's where Dad would want me. I called an executive meeting for ten o'clock. Please be sure the Carroll Boardroom is available. And later, I'd like to meet with the coaches."

"No one would think less of you—"

"Please stop." I took a deep breath. "We have a game on Sunday. I have a lot to learn, and staying home won't accomplish that."

We both turned to the sound of a knock.

It was Grant knocking on the outer office door-frame. "Vee, I'm here to continue our conversation."

I crossed my arms over my breasts. "Our conversation is completed."

He walked past me to my open office door. "I'll be in here."

Clenching my teeth, I turned to Jen. "Five minutes. If we're not done, come in." I nodded toward her watch. "Five minutes. Not a second longer."

She nodded and reaching for my arm, she lowered the volume of her voice. "Are the rumors true?"

My neck stiffened. "Rumors?"

"You're the new owner and CEO?"

That wasn't the rumor I expected, but honestly, I was better prepared to answer that than a question about Fin and me. "I don't know what's official. I'm meeting later today with Dad's attorney and Cammy Wilcox from Coopers' legal."

Jen squeezed my arm. "We all have faith in you, Vee."

Exhaling, I tried to smile. "I appreciate that." I looked at her watch and back to her eyes. "Five minutes."

Jen nodded.

Once inside my office, I closed the door and placed my leather satchel on the floor near my desk. Instead of joining Grant at my small conference table, I took the leather chair behind my desk. "If you want to talk, you'll need to come over here."

Exhaling, Grant stood. The muscles of his cheeks were pulled taut as were the tendons in his neck. Sitting in one of the chairs opposite my desk, he adjusted his suit coat and leaned back. "You and Fin...?" The indication of a question was in his tone.

"Fin and I have a history. You asked about it during the first preseason home game."

"History. Not present or future?"

I laid my arms on the top of my desk and sighed. "What the fuck difference does this make?"

My cousin's eyes closed momentarily as his nostrils flared. "Uncle Reid didn't sign the new will. You know that, right?"

"I was informed."

"How the fuck is the organization supposed to spin the fact that the new owner is fucking our quarterback?"

"As I told you earlier, don't. Don't spin it." I pushed my chair back and stood, my palms slapping my skirt-covered thighs. "Don't address the rumors. If we don't give this story oxygen, it'll die."

Grant narrowed his eyes. "Did Uncle Reid know?"

Tilting my head, I pressed my lips together. "What Dad and I talked about is really none of your damn business. Be at the executive meeting at ten o'clock."

He stood and leaned toward me. "You're not ready

to take over as CEO. The will gives you ownership. Family can fight that. Dad has a copy of the drafted will."

His words cut in a way I wasn't prepared to evaluate.

"However," Grant went on, "it's the Coopers board of directors who are responsible for appointing the CEO."

Clenching my teeth, I met his stare. "Our board of directors will be everyone in the room during the meeting. As owner, I'll lead the board. We can discuss the particulars after I have my say."

"Uncle Reid had that will drawn up when you were eleven years old. Eleven," Grant repeated the number louder. "Do you think that Uncle Reid intended for you to be owner and CEO at eleven?"

"What I know is that it appears Dad had more faith in his eleven-year-old daughter than in anyone else in this organization. News flash. I'm no longer eleven years old."

A knock came to the door, and it opened. Jen stepped inside. "I'm sorry to interrupt you, Vee, but Cammy Wilcox is on line one."

"Thank you, Jen." I turned to Grant. "I'll see you soon."

Exhaling, he turned and walked past Jen.

"Is Cammy really on line one?"

"She is," Jen said.

"Thank you."

"Can I get you some coffee?"

I sighed. "Yes. That would be great."

Exhaling, I scooped my skirt beneath my legs and sat back on my chair. After another cleansing breath, I picked up the receiver of the telephone on my desk. "Cammy, hi. Vee here."

"Thank you for taking my call."

"We're still meeting this afternoon, aren't we?"

"We are. I debated about talking to you before then." She sighed. "I decided that my job is as legal counsel for the Coopers, not individuals."

She had my attention. "Is there something I need to know about the Coopers?"

"During the night, I justified that by calling as someone concerned about the future of the Coopers, ergo, I had the right to make this call."

Nibbling on my lower lip, I replied, "I'm not sure what you're saying."

"Vee, I recommend you seek your own legal counsel."

The feeling of dread returned to the pit of my stomach. "Joseph Eads?"

"This is off the record."

"Okay," I replied.

"After you left Mrs. Hubbard's home last evening, there was a discussion. It seems that there are various opinions on your ability to take over as CEO."

"I just had a visit from Grant."

Cammy exhaled. "So you know that they want to stop you from being CEO?"

"I do now. Can they?"

"The long and short of it is they can try."

Closing my eyes, I tilted my head back.

Cammy went on, "I don't think they will succeed."

My mind swam with the meaning behind Cammy's information. My own family was plotting against me. I'd told Dad I wouldn't cut out family. It seemed they wanted to cut me out.

"How can I stop them?"

"This isn't about you stopping them. It's about them trying to stop you. I read case law and have concluded that the Coopers have one owner. That owner is now you. If the drafted will had gone into effect, the structure would be different. It didn't. A drafted unsigned will is about as binding as an agreement written on a cocktail napkin.

"As sole owner, you have the ultimate authority. You could name yourself as CEO or you could hire a qualified individual. The decision is solely yours."

"It's not up to the executive board?"

"Vee, you are sole owner. You could dismiss the entire board and bring in new people. You have full authority. I'm concerned," she went on, "that you are about to be ambushed. Without proper legal counsel, let's just say...I'm worried. Vee, Reid had faith in you.

His reasons to change his will were more about the guilt that he carried."

"Guilt?"

"He felt Rachel was unfairly left out of the Coopers' franchise. That carries on to her children."

"You're saying that Dad wanted to right a wrong he felt that my grandfather made?"

"Yes," Cammy replied. "Do you have someone in mind to represent you?"

"I don't." I thought about it. "Leigh is a public defender and an interested party—she can't defend me. I've always had faith in Dad's choices."

"I specialize in corporate law. I have the name of a personal-estate attorney. She's good and deals with clients with substantial wealth. If you decide to call her, you can tell her that I recommended her."

My mind was swirling. "The personal attorney will be able to help me with Dad's will, but what about the meeting today? If my own family ambushes me?"

Cammy was silent for a moment. "I can join you for the executive meeting. I'm not there to represent you, but for the Coopers."

"Thanks, Cammy," I said, "that would make me feel better. Also, please give me the estate lawyer's information."

I wrote down the name, Tricia Loften, and the name and phone number of her law firm. As I hung up, Jen returned with my coffee. "Here you go."

"Thank you. I have some calls to make. Please don't let anyone interrupt me."

Jen stiffened her neck. "Coach Tilson is outside. I told him you were on a call."

"Tell him I'll meet with him later in the day."

"He said it won't take long."

"All right, send him in."

CHAPTER 12

Vee

Coach Don Tilson was in his eleventh year with the Coopers organization. Dad and Royce Beasley, the general manager, first hired him as a defensive line coach. He moved up to defensive coordinator, and five years ago, he was named head coach, replacing Everington. While we had winning seasons with Tilson and Beasley as the public faces of football operations, the last two had been the most successful. Last year the Coopers made it to the conference championship, our best run of Dad's tenure. The Coopers played in the Super Bowl in the late 1990s under Grandpa Carroll. It was Royce Beasley's first year with the team.

That achievement cemented Beasley's longer-than-usual time as a general manager. Despite his first-year success, the Coopers have never again made it to the Super Bowl.

"Vee," the coach said, entering my office.

In his mid-fifties, Tilson was a handsome, rugged-looking man who gave off the air of superiority and indifference. He was known for brutal press conferences after a loss and being only slightly more polite after a win.

"Coach" —I gestured toward the chair beyond my desk— "please have a seat."

Unlike Grant in his custom suit, Coach Tilson was wearing blue jeans and a Coopers pullover. His small pudge of a belly showed that while he knew the best conditioning and moves for the team, he didn't regularly partake in the workouts himself.

He exhaled. "I'm sorry..."

I shook my head. "We all are. We need to concentrate on the next game, not the past."

Tilson pressed his lips together and nodded. "That's why I'm here. Every Monday morning, before we show film and work with the team, I would meet Reid in his office. We'd drink a cup of coffee and discuss the game. It was an unofficial meeting, never scheduled. No one took notes. We simply talked."

"I didn't know that."

"It was our time to make sure we were on the same page." He inhaled and leaned forward. "Last night, it hit me that we didn't get that time yesterday."

A lump of emotion formed in my throat that I tried to swallow. I knew what he was feeling. Dad and I were supposed to meet yesterday morning.

"That's why I'm here, Vee. You're now the owner. I spoke with Andrew Pratt and Darius Brown about your work this season in learning plays."

"I don't think I'll have time for that..." I began.

"They were both impressed." A small smile cracked his veneer. "And let's be honest, they aren't easy men to impress."

"Thank you. That means a lot."

"The thing is," Tilson went on, "the players—all of them—are also impressed by your presence at practices and games."

I caught his addition of "all players," wondering if it was referencing Fin in some way.

"I don't know. There's a lot I don't know."

Tilson straightened his neck. "I could be gone tomorrow. I know that. It's how this game and career choice goes. What Reid did for the franchise can't be learned overnight. You don't have to listen to me, but I would like you to consider maintaining your presence. If you show the players that the Coopers will go on, they'll believe it."

"And all the other things Dad did?"

"Darin or Rachel would know the most."

It was my turn to inhale and sit taller. "Thank you, Coach. I have many things to consider. I would like to meet with you and all the coaches this afternoon."

"We'll be happy to meet with you." He stared for a minute. "Tell me your thoughts on Sunday's win against the Cardinals."

Leaning back and puckering my lips, I exhaled. "I-I." I hadn't thought about the game since Sunday, but that wasn't what an owner should say. Clearing the cobwebs in my mind, I thought back to Sunday. Sitting forward, I gripped the armrests of my chair. "Our offense was good."

"Good?"

"Not great. Play calling was too conservative in my opinion. The Cardinals' defense was reading our plays. Especially when Pratt had Simpson on the field. He only had a three and out. His drive ended with a punt."

"What about Graham?"

"He had an eighty-eight-yard touchdown in the beginning of the game," I said without changing my expression. "We've seen Graham throw the ball down-field, yet it was as if after we had points on the board, Pratt only called prevent offense—short shuffle passes, handoffs, and short runs. He kept the clock running, but when the Cardinals' quarterback threw that Hail Mary in the third, our lead was cut in half."

Coach Tilson nodded. "You would have called different plays?"

I mustered a small smile. "I'm not on the sidelines

to make calls or micromanage. I'm there to learn and discuss. We're discussing."

"Defense?"

"Saved the game. Malik's interception in the fourth quarter was the play that swung the momentum solidly in our favor."

Tilson smiled and stood. "I'm looking forward to our talk next Monday."

"Is that the way you talked with Dad? Because it seemed like you were listening more than talking."

"I'm doing both. You were paying attention on the sideline."

"Of course."

Tilson nodded. "One more thing...?"

I also stood, maintaining eye contact. "Yes?"

"There's a rumor."

"I seem to recall my dad saying that rumors are carried by haters, spread by fools, and accepted by idiots. We don't have any haters, fools, or idiots on the Coopers..." I arched my eyebrows. "Do we?"

"No, ma'am, we don't."

"I'll look forward to our Monday morning unscheduled meetings."

His grin quirked. "Seven sharp."

"Oh," I said with a scoff. "Early."

Tilson's grin disappeared. "Reid was always waiting for me, until yesterday."

"Until yesterday."

As Tilson walked away, I thought about all he said. Without my discussion with Grant and Cammy, I could have taken everything at face value. Tilson genuinely enjoyed the unscheduled meetings with Dad. Pratt and Brown said complimentary things about my work on the sidelines. Tilson felt my presence would be beneficial for all players, and he listened to my thoughts on our last game.

It was his comment about Uncle Darin or Aunt Rachel.

Is Tilson being nice or was he working for me to abdicate the position of CEO?

After Coach was gone, I removed my phone from my bag. I'd missed multiple calls; some were from family and friends. There was another call from Preston and multiple from unidentified numbers. Deciding I wasn't ready to tackle any of those phone calls, I was about ready to lay my phone on the desk, when it vibrated with an incoming text message. The screen read *Fin.*

"HOW ARE YOU DOING?"

A smile curled my lips as I texted back.

. . .

"OH, YOU KNOW, ANOTHER DAY IN PARADISE."

"REMEMBER TO THINK ABOUT OUR KISS IF YOUR DAY GOES SOUTH."

OUR KISS. I wished that could be my main thought. Instead of texting back, I sent a smile with a heart for lips emoji.

I ARRIVED to the Carroll meeting room about fifteen minutes early.

Aunt Rachel was present. "Vee," she said, "I invited Bre Stanton to this meeting."

I nodded a closed-lip smile to Dad's assistant. "Why?" I asked Aunt Rachel.

"Because if anyone knows what your father did on a daily basis, it would be Bre."

Exhaling, I took the seat at the head of the table. "That's an excellent idea. Bre, can you tell me about Dad's Monday-morning meetings with Coach Tilson?"

"They happened before I was in the office. Every Monday following a game, I'd get to the office and they'd either be talking, saying goodbye, or there would be two coffee cups in the kitchen."

Her story supported Tilson's.

Over the years, Dad made remarks about Bre being a great assistant. He often spoke of her abilities. In her early forties, Bre was also an understated beauty. While they were both slender, in every other way she was the opposite of Daphne. Bre had a runner's body. I couldn't recall a time I'd seen her with much in the way of makeup or flashy clothes. "I know Dad thought the world of you, Bre."

She dabbed her eyes with a tissue. "I'm sorry for being emotional."

"We need to focus on keeping the Coopers running the same as they would if Dad were still here."

Bre nodded and pushed a folder in my direction. "Last night, Mrs. Marsh called and asked me to put together Mr. Hubbard's weekly schedule."

I took the folder. "You don't have this all on your computer?"

"I do. Mr. Hubbard liked paper. He said when he could hold something it was tangible—real."

I opened the folder. The document was prepared as if Bre had copied pages from a daily planner. I began to read. My smiling facial expression didn't match the fresh tears flowing down my cheeks. I looked up at Aunt Rachel. "Do you have a copy?"

She nodded.

"What do you think?"

"I think Reid will be missed. I also think that Bre is essential for helping the next CEO."

"You don't think that should be me?"

Aunt Rachel looked around. It was still the three of us. "I think that you're capable, Vee. It seems to me that midseason isn't the best time for a change of owner and CEO." Before I could speak, she lifted her hand. "I also know we don't have a choice. As Reid's sister and your aunt, I'd like you to consider that you could assign the job of CEO to someone else on a temporary basis."

That was similar to what Coach Tilson said.

Aunt Rachel went on. "And maybe that person could work with you so that you're able to take over the position in the future."

"Dad said you wanted to retire."

"I told him that during preseason. I'm getting old and I'd like to enjoy life. Maybe travel and not for football games."

I nodded. "When?"

My aunt sighed. "I told Reid I wanted to retire following the postseason." She tilted her head. "I'm willing to work a little longer."

"You're essential with football operations."

"The reason I asked Bre for this information was because my assistant, Millie Jones, is capable of doing my work. Similar to Bre, she's been with the franchise for many years." Aunt Rachel's green eyes met mine. "Am I interviewing for the temporary position?"

"Do you believe I have that power?"

She inhaled and leaned back. "Who spoke with you?"

"Grant."

Aunt Rachel swallowed. "Vee, Reid loved you. Do I wish he'd signed the new will? Yes. As a matter of fact, he and Darin were in a heated discussion during the last game. The reality is Reid didn't sign. You, Maeve, are now the owner, just like Reid was when our father passed away. At that time, Reid and I were co-vice presidents. I was football and he was business." She shook her head. "You know our history."

"I do."

The door opened and others joined us.

CHAPTER 13

Fin

The delicious aroma of homemade vegetable lasagna roasting in the oven filled Vee's condominium. A Caesar salad sat chilling in the refrigerator, and a bottle of uncorked wine was breathing on the counter. The wine was a new bottle of *Dangerous*, the bourbon-barrel-aged semi-sweet red wine from Versailles, Kentucky, that Vee had opened for us the night of our disastrous and necessary quarrel. When I left that evening, it felt as if there was no chance for the two of us to find our way back together. Now, in retrospect, that discussion was exactly what we both needed to begin on our road to finding one another again.

Two people experienced the same breakup, and yet their points of view were miles apart. My thoughts went back to our time together in college. Vee was right; I would have treated her differently if I had known who her father was. At the same time, I missed out on knowing the real Reid Hubbard.

Ours was a relationship that could never be, not now.

While Coach Tilson told us to spend the day mourning, what he meant was for each of us to exorcise our own ghosts when it came to Reid Hubbard. As I spent the day retrieving things from my apartment as well as grocery shopping—all under a different baseball cap, I thought a lot about the man we just lost.

I didn't know Reid Hubbard in a meaningful way— I hadn't been given that opportunity. My guess was that most of the Coopers' players never knew him personally. We knew him as the owner of the team where we played. We knew him as the man across the table during contract negotiations, the man at the desk in the head office, and the man watching us from a suite high in Crystal Light Stadium. He was successful as an NFL CEO and owner. During his tenure with the Coopers, he managed to build a new stadium and a winning record.

As the day progressed, I realized that beyond a player's perspective, Reid Hubbard must have also been a great father. Vee's love and admiration for him spoke volumes.

Reid Hubbard and the Coopers' GM, Royce

Beasley, were the reason I was here in Lexington. I owed both gratitude for taking a chance on me, especially after the last shitty year with LA. Without their faith, I wouldn't be standing in Maeve's condo, preparing our dinner, and waiting for her arrival.

A smile lifted my cheeks. If Vee had her way back in September, I wouldn't have been signed by the Coopers. Peering upward, I spoke aloud. "Thank you, Mr. Hubbard. You're the reason I'm here. Now, if she'll let me, I promise to take good care of your daughter."

My nerves were taut as I worried about Vee.

I checked my phone again. The last text message I received from Vee said that she was almost done at Daphne's house. The funeral preparations were complete. Earlier, she'd texted saying there were reporters outside the gate at Crystal Light and at the gate of Daphne's property.

Thankfully, things had changed for the better at the Vine. This building was inhabited by wealthy Lexington residents. It didn't take long for the residents to complain about the crowds on the first floor. This morning, management took much-appreciated actions for the privacy of their residents. There were now velvet ropes, a black cloth screen, and a security guard stationed at the elevator on the first floor.

Residents could travel up and down the elevator, especially from the underground parking garage, without fear of seeing their picture on social media. That was true of visitors too. I had my keycard at the ready, waiting for Vee's text. Staying away from her all day long had been its own kind of torture.

How is she battling her sadness?

What happened today at Maker's Mark?

Are reporters still hounding her?

What about her family?

The questions continued to come and go like waves on a sandy beach. One question would seem monumental, a tsunami, and then it would disappear and another would arrive.

Has she been having to deal with the fallout of this morning's scandalous story?

There was no doubt this morning the story with my picture bothered me more than it seemed to bother Vee. She probably figured she didn't have the bandwidth to take on another possible catastrophe. That didn't mean others wouldn't react. Honestly, all day I expected a call from Coach Tilson. He'd specifically warned the players to be on their best behavior, saying anything we do will reflect on the team. Rumors of a relationship between the new owner and a player would certainly qualify as a distraction that could cast the Coopers in a bad light.

The call never came. The only person outside of me and Vee who had spoken about it was my agent,

Jackson Blanch. If any of my teammates were curious about the social media insinuations, they were holding their questions for tomorrow's locker room.

My phone buzzed and danced across the countertop. Vee's name was on the screen.

"Are you on your way home?" I asked in lieu of a greeting.

"Mr. Graham?"

The deep voice was male and unfamiliar. I pulled the phone away from my ear to be certain it was Vee's name on the screen. It was. I gripped the phone tighter. "This is Mr. Graham. Where's Ms. Hubbard?"

"Sir, she's safe. My name is Deputy Ellis, from the Fayette County Sheriff's Department."

My heart rate elevated to an unhealthy level. "Sheriff's Department. Vee... is safe?" My volume rose. "Where is she?" I searched frantically for my keys. Forget dinner, I needed to get to her. Finding them on the table near the door, I bolted into the hallway.

The phone was still to my ear.

"There was an incident outside the Hubbard property. Ms. Hubbard was unharmed. Unfortunately, Ms. Hubbard left her phone in her car at the scene. Deputy Pittman is driving her home. He called and said Ms. Hubbard asked me to call you."

"She's on her way home?" I stopped as I was about to push the button for the elevator.

"Yes, sir."

"Why isn't Vee with her car? What happened?" I asked.

"The deputy on patrol at the Hubbards' gate was called away. He wasn't present when Ms. Hubbard attempted to exit the property."

"Attempted?" I clenched my teeth. "Reporters?"

"My information is preliminary. The incident is under investigation. We're reviewing security footage and taking eyewitness statements. What we know for certain is that Ms. Hubbard drove her car off the road into a ravine. The deputy arrived moments later."

A ravine?

Reporters.

They were out of hand.

What the fuck?

As I walked back toward Vee's place, my thoughts went to the first floor and more reporters. Velvet ropes and a black screen wouldn't protect her if she walked through the lobby. "Please tell the deputy to take Ms. Hubbard inside the parking garage. I'll be down there."

"The parking garage. Why?"

Because I fucking told you to. I couldn't say that. Instead, I took a deep breath. "There have been reporters on the first floor. From the garage, I can get her back to her condo. You're certain that she's not hurt?"

"She's shaken, but Ms. Hubbard insisted on leaving the scene and not waiting for an ambulance."

I shook my head with a little bit of a grin. That's my Vee. "She can be stubborn." I opened the door and entered the condo.

"Mr. Graham, I'll contact Deputy Pittman. You can expect them in under ten minutes."

"Thank you."

CHAPTER 14

Fin

Throwing my key fob on the table, I made my way back to the kitchen. Leaning against the counter for support, I tried to make sense of what occurred as a concoction of emotions surged through my circulation. The worries and concerns from earlier in the day were superseded by the new information. "Fucking reporters," I said to the empty room.

The deputy would be taking Vee to the garage. Suddenly, I worried that the police car wouldn't be able to enter. Yesterday, when Jacob escorted us down to the garage, he gave me a card with the number for the concierge desk. I pulled it from my wallet and called.

"Ethan," I said, "this is Griffin Graham from number 706. I need your assistance..."

The garage was chilly at this time in the evening. With my arms crossed over my chest and my foot bouncing impatiently, I waited for the sheriff's car. Ethan was at the gate, ready to allow the sheriff's vehicle to enter the garage. That kid and Jacob both deserved bonuses for all the extra work they were doing for us.

I tried to keep my thoughts from turning dark as I imagined the scene outside the Hubbard property. What happened? Why did Vee run off the road? Where was the deputy?

Security.

That was what Vee needed.

We'd hire private security.

Headlights brought my focus back to the present. I held my breath as I watched a car enter—a blue Jeep. Not a sheriff's car. Turning away from the driver, I paced the length of two parking spaces until the car passed.

Another set of headlights shone from the entrance. My chest tightened like a fist.

Fayette County Sheriff's Department was written on the side of the vehicle. I lifted my hand to shield my eyes from the bright illumination. Every muscle in my body pulled taut as the car came to a stop. Squinting, I tried to look through the windows.

Only the deputy was visible in the front seat. That meant Vee was in the back seat. In two strides I was there. Opening the rear passenger door, I scanned the gorgeous woman in the back seat. She was stoically calm, considering what she'd been through. Moisture glistened in her green eyes. I offered her my hand.

Vee stepped from the car without saying a word. She wrapped her arms around my torso and buried her face in my shirt. Instinctively, I encircled her body with my arm—a shield to keep her safe. With my other hand, I splayed my fingers over the soft satin of her blouse and held her against me. "Are you okay?"

"I am now." Her words were muffled.

Deputy Pittman cleared his throat, popping our bubble. While Vee pulled away, I kept my touch in the small of her back, unwilling to let her get away from me. "Deputy, thank you for getting Ms. Hubbard home safely."

He nodded. "Ms. Hubbard, once again, I'm going to recommend you see a doctor."

Vee inhaled. "I'm fine. Seeing a doctor doesn't fit with my schedule. I'll have someone look me over tomorrow at the football center. What about my phone and my car?"

"Deputy Ellis retrieved your phone and bag."

Vee looked from side to side. "My bag. Oh my. I obviously wasn't thinking. Thank you."

I wrapped my arm around her shoulders and pulled her closer. "Do we need to pick them up?"

"No, sir. He will bring them here."

"Thank you."

"And your car," he said, "will be towed to the dealership off Highway 25. We may need to ask you more questions about what happened. Are you available?"

"I will do my best," Vee said. "Right now, I just want to get upstairs."

"We'll be in touch," Deputy Pittman said as he walked back to the sheriff's vehicle.

Palming Vee's cheeks, I drank in her emerald-green eyes. "Are you all right?"

She nodded. "I can tell you more once we're upstairs."

We turned the corner and found Ethan waiting for us by the elevator. As we rode up to the seventh floor, I told him that a sheriff's deputy would be bringing Ms. Hubbard's belongings soon. Ethan assured us that he would receive them and bring them upstairs. Vee remained silent, her lips paling from the pressure as she held them tightly together.

Once we were alone and safe behind the locked outer door of her condominium, I let out a long breath. The worry throughout the day and panic instilled by the call from a sheriff's deputy had me wanting to move, to pounce and attack. None of that would help Vee.

"Fin? What smells so good?" she asked.

In the light of the kitchen, I saw her more clearly. Gently, I lifted my fingers to her cheek. "Fuck, Vee. You're bruised."

She inclined her face to my touch. "I don't know how it looks. I haven't seen myself."

I scanned her up and down. "Is there more? How did you get hurt?"

"The airbags deployed." She shook her head and looked down. "My skirt...there was powder..." She lifted her hands and splayed her fingers. "I only knew my hands were sore."

I took her hands in mine. They were ice cold and the skin was red and inflamed. "Tell me what happened."

Quickly, Vee blinked her eyes, fighting back new tears. "It happened fast and at the same time, it was slow motion." She exhaled and laid a hand on her stomach. "I think I need to sit."

Reaching for her slender waist, I lifted her to the kitchen island.

A slight smile spread across her lips. "You don't have to be a caveman. I could have sat in a chair."

"I could pound my chest if you'd like." I leaned closer and tipped my forehead to hers. "We don't have time for a chair. I need to know what happened and why you're injured."

"I'm not injured."

I lifted her hands, turning them so that we could both see the red and puffy abrasions. "We can argue or you can talk. It was reporters, wasn't it?"

Vee nodded. "There has always been a sheriff's car at Dad's gate, I mean, since yesterday. It wasn't there when I tried to leave. I didn't realize it was missing until the gate started to open."

The trembling of her hands filled me with rage. "What the fuck did they do?"

She shook her head. "They came onto the property. I tried to drive. I made it outside the gate but stopped to be sure no one stayed inside the property." She took a stuttered breath. "It was like they came from everywhere and swarmed the car. I honked the horn and tried to move forward. They were yelling questions at me. I decided to keep driving slowly, hoping they'd back away. When they did, I realized the road was blocked with another vehicle." She looked down at her hands and back up. "I turned the wheel to avoid it, and I guess I hit the accelerator. My car went forward and down." She rubbed her left shoulder. "The seat belt pulled tight and the airbags exploded." Her eyes met mine. "I wasn't going fast at first. I just wanted to get away from them."

"Was anyone injured? Did you hit anyone?"

"No." She shook her head. "I don't think so. The deputy arrived right after I went off the road. I don't know where the people all went. They dispersed."

"Cowards," I said. "I'm so sorry."

Vee looked up at me. Her expression brought back my earlier rage.

"Fin, I'm tired."

I nodded. "You're so strong, Vee."

She blinked away tears. "I'm tired of being strong."

"Then let me do it. Let me take charge."

A faint shade of pink returned color to her cheeks. "Please."

There were so many things I wanted to know; however, Vee was my priority. "I have one important question."

"What is it?" she asked.

"Dinner first or bath?"

Her lips curled as she exhaled. "Whatever is cooking smells wonderful. I've never come home to such an amazing aroma. What is it?"

"Lasagna."

Her eyes opened wide.

"Not to worry, it's vegetable." I tugged her skirt higher on her thighs and stepped between her knees.

Vee lifted her hands to my shoulders. "All the way home, in the back of that car, I kept thinking what it would be like to arrive to an empty condo, to be all alone..."

"You're not alone, Vee. I'm here." My lips landed on hers. For a slice of time the world around us no longer mattered. We kissed and kissed, our heads turning, our tongues swirling, and our breathing shallowing. Soft mews filled the air as she pressed her breasts against me.

When we pulled apart, Vee's hands lowered, her fingers splaying over my chest. "Your heart is beating fast."

I laid my hand over her breastbone. "And yours is beating. When I first answered the call and it wasn't you, I was scared that we lost you too."

"I'm here and I'm safe."

Stepping back, I lifted one of her sexy legs and removed her shoe. Next, I did the same for the other foot. Reaching behind her, I tugged at the zipper on her skirt.

"Fin."

"You should be comfortable." I winked. "Remember, I'm in charge. You can relax."

CHAPTER 15

Vee

I scooted off the counter. As my feet hit the floor, Fin scooped me up and lifted me to his chest.

"Dinner can wait."

Part of me wanted to argue. There was another part of me, the part that told him how tired I was of being strong, that kept my protests at bay. That confession was the most honest thing I'd said all day, maybe in my entire life. As he carried me through the condominium, I laid my head against his chest. The steady rhythm of his heart soothed my aching temples. His warmth disappeared as Fin gently lowered me to the bed. The mattress dipped as he sat at my side.

"I need to see you, Vee. I need to know you're not truly harmed."

I lifted my hands. "My hands…"

He shook his head. "All of you." The intensity of his blue stare soothed and excited me in equal portions. I didn't object as Fin pulled my skirt down, the one he'd unzipped in the kitchen. I lifted my arms as he removed my blouse. His laser-focused vision scanned every inch of my exposed flesh. I winced as he gently probed the skin of my left shoulder.

"I fucking hate seeing your beautiful skin bruised."

I grinned. "Unless it's my wrists."

There was no humor in his expression. "Stand up for me. I want to see all of you."

Sighing in resignation, I moved my legs and my feet from the bed to the floor. As I stood before him, I was bathed in his concerned and possessive stare. The ferocity filled me with confidence and I unclasped my bra, allowing the straps to fall down my arms. Next, I snagged the waist of my panties and allowed them to drop to the floor.

"Turn around."

My hesitation was only for a moment before I did as he commanded. Slowly, I turned one complete circle and then a second. Fin reached for my hands, pulling me between his spread knees. He removed the tie from my hair, allowing my locks to flow over my shoulders.

Fin's kisses began on my fingers, then over my sore knuckles. He didn't stop, moving up my arms to my collarbone and lower. A trail of goose bumps formed in his wake. My nipples painfully hardened as they became the focus of his attention.

My head lobbed back.

This was a dream.

After the last few days, my mind had given up on reality. I was floating in a sea of sensations. My core twisted and my knees wobbled. I steadied myself by placing my hands on Fin's shoulders. All at once, my world shifted, landing me back on the soft mattress.

The scent of sandalwood filled my senses as Fin spread my knees and his lips roamed from my breasts to my stomach, and lower to my pussy. Lightning bolts of electricity raced through me. My hips bucked and my back arched. I reached for his soft hair, wordlessly begging for more.

This was more than allowing Fin to take charge, it was a cleansing and rebirth all in one. The emotions I'd worked hard throughout the day to subdue found an outlet as I shouted his name. The bedroom filled with the sounds of ecstasy and desire. My moans became higher pitched as fireworks exploded behind my eyelids.

I pulled him higher, wanting and needing this surrender—the closeness of two people so intertwined we didn't know where one began and the other ended. I called out as Fin filled me in the most delicious way. As he moved, claiming me and recentering my world, I arched my back as his lips found mine. For a moment in time, the despair of the world and the deception of my family was forgotten. My every thought was consumed with the man above me, dominating me, and loving me.

The sounds we made were the same as those echoed through centuries of lovemaking. High-pitched treble clef and guttural lower pitched bass clef. Our bodies united with heady breaths, skin against skin. Giving my mind and body over to Fin freed me of the weight I was required to carry. Hundreds of pounds evaporated, opening my lungs to the warm air only he could give.

No longer a chorus clatter, Fin's words of comfort and declarations of love filled a void my father's passing had created. His phrases of confidence and knowledge of my dedication and commitment were like rain to cracked, dry soil. I drank them in—each one—as nourishment to my battered self-esteem.

Detonation after detonation set my nervous system ablaze. Fin's movements came quicker, each thrust impossibly deeper as the air filled with his deep baritone growl.

He stayed above me, his weight over me as his lips found mine. With our noses only millimeters apart, his eyes swirled with emotion. "I fucking love you, Vee. I've been worried about you all day."

I wanted to tell him that he needn't worry, but instead, I pushed my reflex response away. "I love you.

I'm so glad you were here." I tilted my head. "I'm not used to anyone worrying about me."

"Get used to it."

My cheeks rose with a genuine smile. "I'll try."

Breaking our connection, Fin rolled to my side. I followed, lifting my head to his hard shoulder, my fingertips swirling his chest hair. "When did you take off your clothes?"

"I don't know."

The room filled with needed laughter.

"I thought you preferred the power play."

"You relinquished yours when you said I was in charge." He kissed my nose. "What did you and Daphne decide about your dad's service?"

"It will be a week from today."

"Tuesday?"

I nodded. "That way the coaches and team can attend. We have a bye the next weekend..." I sighed. "It won't be open to the public, but Daphne and I agreed that Dad thought of the Coopers as family."

Fin's lips brushed over mine. "Now, I think you should soak in a warm bath. However sore you are now, you'll be ten times worse tomorrow."

I pushed out my lower lip. "I was hoping for a taste of that delicious-smelling lasagna."

"Then you'll have both."

"Both?"

A few minutes later, I was submerged in warm

water with muscle-healing bath salts. Fin promised they worked, and as a man who got beat up for a living, I believed him. Steam rose from the water as I lay back. In front of me was a bamboo bath tray I hadn't used in ages. And on the tray was a glass of *Dangerous* semi-sweet wine and a Caesar salad.

The bathroom door opened and Fin entered with two plates and silverware.

A giggle bubbled from my throat. "I can honestly say I've never eaten dinner in the bathtub before."

"Me either." He set the plate and silverware on the tray. His meal was now on the vanity. "Your dinner is served."

Quickly, I sat up, cut into the layered slice of lasagna, and brought the fork to my lips. A hum of satisfaction filled the air. "This is delicious." I looked up at him. He was wearing basketball shorts and nothing else. I knew that for a fact because I watched him dress. "Did you actually make this from scratch?"

"I didn't make the noodles, but I put all the ingredients together." He came closer. "I think that tray is big enough for both plates."

My eyebrows quirked. "Are you going to join me?"

"I'm fairly certain we'll both fit."

I watched Fin with overwhelming appreciation. "If this is what it means to let you be in charge, I'm signing up for more."

"You may not realize it, but you signed up for a life-time plan."

Moving my plate, I made room for his and moved my wine glass to the counter at the side of the tub. It was as Fin began to remove his shorts that the doorbell rang.

"Oh," I pouted. "I like watching you undress."

"It's probably your phone and bag."

"How could I forget about those things?" Before he could answer, I replied to my own question. "I think it's because you're a master at distraction."

"Hold that thought," he said before slipping out of the bathroom.

I was suddenly ravenous. No doubt the garlicky aroma, variety of vegetables, noodles, and white sauce were at fault. Each bite melted in my mouth as I consumed the lasagna and salad. While I hadn't thought about food during the day, I realized the last meal I'd eaten was breakfast.

My plate was almost empty when Fin returned. His earlier expression was gone. His muscular chest was covered with a gray t-shirt, and he was carrying my terrycloth bathrobe.

"What's wrong?"

"A state police officer and a detective are here. They insist on talking to you." Fin lifted the bamboo tray.

CHAPTER 16

Vee

"State police officer?"

Fin nodded. "And a detective. Ethan brought them up with your bag and phone. He apologized, saying he couldn't call ahead because he had your phone."

The water sloshed as I stood, the silky moisture rolling down my nude body. "What's this about?"

"I don't know for sure. They only said they want to speak with you."

Fin offered me his hand. As I stepped out of the tub, he wrapped a fluffy towel around me. "I told him you were indisposed." His displeasure with our interruption was evident by his clenched jaw and tightened muscles on the side of his face. "I'll go out there and wait with them." He kissed the top of my head. "Don't hurry."

"Is it about tonight's accident or Dad?"

"We'll find out when you're ready."

Shivering, I turned toward the large mirror over the vanity, taking in my reflection. Instinctively, my fingers went to the discoloration on my right cheek and I grimaced. I couldn't explain why my right cheek took more of the airbag's brunt than the left. My only guess was that I must have turned my head as the bag exploded. Using a separate towel, I patted dry the ends of my hair before twisting the length into a messy bun on the top of my head.

Stepping into the bedroom, I paused at the sight of clothes littering the floor and rug near the bed. It appeared as if a tornado had come and gone. Tornado Fin. I felt my smile lifting my cheeks at the memory of Fin taking charge, telling me he had faith in me, and working my body into a frenzy.

I wasn't a person who sought out praise or craved acclaim. Nevertheless, I needed it or wanted it more than I realized. Today's executive meeting was difficult. Closing my eyes, I saw the table filled with family, with people who should be supportive, all voicing their opinion that I wasn't ready to take on the role of CEO. I was inexperienced, unqualified, and too young. Thank goodness for Cammy. She stopped Grant and Uncle

Darin cold when they mentioned contesting Dad's will in court.

The will, she stated, was old, but there wasn't a legal requirement for people to update their will. The Coopers were left to Dad's children; being the only one, the team was mine. Whoever fills the position of CEO would be my choice. I felt I deserved the position. However, after listening to their critique, I was starting to believe that the person best suited for CEO wasn't me.

I donned panties, capri leggings, and a soft large Coopers sweatshirt. Slipping my feet into an old pair of crocs, I took a deep breath and tried to keep my hands from shaking as I opened the door. The sound of men's voices reverberated from down the hall, not in a loud way but simply at a conversational decibel.

"Ms. Hubbard," the man in uniform said, standing. His eyes opened wide. "Mr. Graham mentioned that you were in a car accident today." He nodded toward my face. "Do you have any other injuries?"

Fin stood too, as did another man, white haired and wearing a rumpled sports jacket.

"Yes. Are you here about what happened today?" I walked closer to Fin.

"No, ma'am," the white-haired man said. "We're here in relation to your father's accident."

I exhaled. "Gentlemen, it's late, and I've had multiple difficult days."

"We're sorry for your loss," the white-haired man said. "I'm Detective Jack Oldson, and this is State Trooper Everett Daniels."

"Do you have a warrant?"

"No, Ms. Hubbard," Detective Oldson said. "We're only here to talk with you." Before I could respond, he went on, "Trooper Daniels worked the scene of your father's accident, and I'm part of the team investigating it. We have a few questions we'd like to ask you."

I furrowed my forehead. "Why are you investigating? It was an accident. That's what I was told."

"When a fatality is involved, it's not that simple," Trooper Daniels explained.

Clenching my jaw, I turned toward my living room. "Please come in and have a seat."

Although every fiber within my being wanted to sit next to Fin—to feel his warmth and support—I chose one of the singular chairs. The others all took seats.

"Ms. Hubbard," the detective began, "are you all right with discussing Mr. Hubbard's case in the presence of Mr. Graham?"

My gaze went toward Fin and back to the detective. "Anything you say to me can be said in front of Griffin."

"Very well." The detective pulled his phone from his pocket. "Ms. Hubbard, are you aware of the medications your father took?"

"I wasn't. I was told that some were found during the autopsy." I tried to think. "Beta blockers, which I believe is for blood pressure." My mind was tired. "I'm sorry. There were others, but I can't remember them."

"The early tests only disclose types of drugs. The others were benzodiazepines and antihistamines."

"I'm familiar with antihistamines, not the other."

"Benzodiazepines," the detective said, "are prescription sedatives, often used for anxiety, insomnia, or alcohol withdrawal."

"Have you spoken to Daphne Hubbard?" I asked. "My father's wife...widow, I guess. She would have a better understanding about Dad's daily routine."

"We have," Detective Oldson said. "According to Mrs. Hubbard, your father only took the beta blockers."

I shook my head. "Why is this important? Maybe Dad had seasonal allergies or trouble sleeping. I don't know." I'd suffered allergies most of my life. Was that hereditary? "Besides, the accident wasn't Dad's fault." I turned toward the state trooper. "Uncle Darin was told by the state police—you—that the accident was caused by a semi-truck that changed lanes too quickly. The driver said he didn't see Dad's car."

"I spoke with the driver," the trooper said. "He was very shaken up."

"He'd just killed my father. I'm sure he was." It was a harsh reply, but my filter had stopped working hours ago.

"The truck driver works for a large distribution company," Detective Oldson said.

I wasn't sure where this was going.

"You've probably heard of them, Security Supply. They transport industrial and MRO products."

"I've heard of them."

The detective continued, "Security Supply wants the accident further investigated. They are contesting the original report and claim your father was at fault, not their driver."

I jumped to my feet. "Why? And why are you telling me this?"

All three men stood. Fin moved to my side. "This is something that should be discussed with the Hubbards' attorneys, not Vee," Fin said.

"Ma'am, we can inform you that as an heir to Mr. Hubbard's estate," Detective Oldson said, "if the prosecutor determines there's enough evidence to pursue a case, you could be named as co-defendant."

"That's ridiculous."

"We have informed Mrs. Daphne Hubbard as well."

My head was spinning as Fin wrapped his arm around my waist and asked, "Are you charging Vee with anything?"

"Not at this time," the detective answered. "We simply have questions."

I turned to Fin, unsure what to say or do.

"Ms. Hubbard," Detective Oldson said, "I'd like to show you a picture and ask you if you're familiar with the item."

"Fine," I said. "Then you can leave."

"This was found in the glove compartment of your father's car."

The picture was on his phone screen. I recognized the item immediately—a small pillbox, silver with a tiny bird on the lid in what looked like a mosaic. I looked up. "It's a pillbox."

"How do you know that?"

"Because I have one just like it."

"Do you have yours here?" the detective asked.

I turned to Fin. "Where's my bag?"

"It's in the kitchen. I'll get it."

"Come with me," I said to everyone as I walked toward the kitchen. My leather bag was on the island counter. Frantically, I began removing items from my bag—my tablet, water bottle, wallet, and hairbrush. I made it down to a few hair ties and pens. "It's not in my purse."

"What do you keep in your pillbox?"

"Benadryl."

The two men looked at one another.

The connection hit me. "Benadryl is an antihistamine. Why are you asking?"

"Did you offer Benadryl to your father?"

"No," I answered immediately. "Mine is over the

counter, you can buy it anywhere—he could buy it anywhere. I haven't really needed it this fall. I just have it—in case."

"But you don't have your pillbox," the detective said.

"Not in my bag, but..." My mind swirled. "I was in an accident earlier today. The sheriff's department returned my bag and phone. The pillbox could have fallen out."

"Do you take any anxiety medication or sleeping pills?"

"No." My neck straightened. "I saw my father for the last time on Sunday afternoon after the Coopers–Cardinals game. He was perfectly healthy. I was supposed to meet with him on Monday. He didn't make the meeting."

"Gentlemen," Fin said, "this has gone on long enough. If you are on a fishing expedition, you'll need to do that with Ms. Hubbard's attorney present."

"Only a few more questions—"

Fin interrupted. "Ms. Hubbard is done answering your questions."

I wrapped my arms around my midsection as Fin walked the two officers to the door. I heard it close and the beeps indicating that Fin activated the security system.

"What the fuck?" he asked as he came back. "Vee, this is ridiculous."

"I didn't give pills to Dad."

Fin wrapped me in his arms and pulled me to his chest. "I know that." He took a step back, still holding onto my shoulders. "Do you have an attorney? One who doesn't represent the Coopers?"

"Cammy gave me a name. I didn't have time to call her today."

"I think you should call first thing tomorrow."

CHAPTER 17

Fin

"I think we made a mistake," Vee said, looking out the passenger side window of my truck. She was gorgeous, dressed in brownish slacks that made her waist look tiny and an amber blouse with flowing sleeves. Her long hair was down, the way I liked it.

"What mistake?"

She turned my way. "I shouldn't be riding with you to Maker's Mark. I should have called for a car. The two of us arriving together is only going to fuel the rumors."

Sunglasses covered her beautiful green eyes as well as the darkening shiner on her right cheek. I also knew that her left shoulder had a purple contusion from the seatbelt, seen this morning as we showered and evidenced by the way she winced when she buckled herself into the truck.

"I have an idea. You can duck down to the floorboard when we pass the reporters."

"If you're trying to be funny, it's not working."

My lips quirked. "I don't know, the idea of you on the floor of my truck is sexy as fuck. A blow job is never a bad way to start a day."

Vee scoffed. "You know, your predilection for oral hasn't changed in fifteen years."

"A man knows what he likes. Besides, I haven't heard you complain."

"This is a ridiculous conversation."

I reached over and squeezed her thigh. "You're right. You'll have to deal with serious shit all day. I'm giving you a few minutes of ridiculousness." I let my hand rest over her leg, unwilling to give up touching her any earlier than necessary. "And the best way to still rumors is to meet them head-on. Rip off the Band-Aid if you will."

She let out a long breath. "Yesterday, I didn't deny or confirm when asked. Hell, you're right. If we admit our relationship and don't make a big deal about it, the rumors will fade away."

"That's our plan?"

She looked at me with an unsure grin. "Yeah, that's our plan."

"If you want to talk about serious shit, I'm serious about you hiring personal security."

Vee pressed her lips together. "I'll have Jen get me a rental car until mine is fixed."

"A rental car won't stop what happened last evening."

Vee exhaled and laid her head on the seat. "I don't plan on going over to Daphne's anytime soon." Her forehead furrowed as she looked up. "Maybe I should look into security for both of us. While the idea of my father's widow driving into a ditch doesn't sadden me too much, Dad would want her to be safe. We can't count on the county and city law enforcement to keep up their watches, and we have no idea how long this paparazzi obsession is going to last." She paused. "Maker's Mark and Crystal Light have security. Uncle Darin said he would increase the number of security officers on duty."

"I like that you included yourself. Your dad would want you safe as well as Daphne."

"It just seems...over the top. My dad was never a flaunt-your-money kind of person." She shrugged. "Daphne, on the other hand..."

"The few times I met him, he seemed low-key."

Vee smiled. "He was."

It was great seeing her be able to talk about her father and be happy. Mourning was a tricky emotion. While I hadn't lost either of my parents, I had lost grandparents. One day the memories brought smiles and the next day, sadness.

"I learned something," she said, "years after it happened. My dad had season tickets at University of Kentucky for football for all the years I worked with the team. That would include when you played. I mean he couldn't be there every weekend, but he was there."

"He was in the stadium?" You would think that it would be at least whispered in the locker room. "No one ever mentioned that."

Her smile was back. "He didn't tell anyone who he was. His seats were in the parent section. He wore a blue Kentucky shirt or sweatshirt and mingled. When he finally told me about it, he said it was fun."

"Why don't you think he told you he was going at the time?"

Vee pursed her lips. "Like you said, Dad was low-key. He didn't want to make me uncomfortable or put me under a spotlight. At the same time, he was being my dad."

Again, I squeezed her thigh. "Keep remembering those happy memories."

"I'd rather think about those than that detective and trooper last night. What they were saying doesn't make sense. We should sue the trucking company, not the other way around."

"I agree that it's fucked," I said. "Talk to the attorney Cammy recommended."

"Her name is Tricia Loften. Her firm is in Frankfort. I'm calling her this morning."

"Good."

Vee sucked in a breath at the sight of news-station vans and people at the gate to Maker's Mark Football Center. "Shit, they're still there."

"My windows are tinted. Just don't look at them."

Vee looked down and covered my hand with hers.

Turning mine palm up, our fingers intertwined.

Vee's grip tightened as I slowed at the gate. Her lower lip disappeared between her teeth as she looked forward and behind. The line to enter Maker's Mark was growing. There were two cars ahead of us and more lining up behind.

"So many people are going to see us," she said.

Reporters were yelling questions.

"What did your meeting with the attorneys discover yesterday?" I asked, suddenly aware that we hadn't talked about it.

"It was Dad's attorney and Cammy. Basically, I'm the official owner. There's a lot of paperwork and legal things, but for the purpose of the Coopers, I'm now the sole owner."

"CEO?" I asked.

"Filling that position is up to me. I can take the reins or hire someone else."

"Who can fire you?" We were the next vehicle up at the gate.

Vee scoffed. "No one."

"Then who cares who sees us?" Releasing Vee's hand, I rolled down my window and spoke to the security officer at the gate. "Griffin Graham."

The man looked down at his tablet and shouted to the other guard, "Open the gate." He turned back to my truck. "Have a good day, Mr. Graham and Ms. Hubbard."

"Shit," Vee mumbled under her breath after we began moving. "He probably follows social media."

"Either that, or he simply recognized you. I can drop you off at the door."

"Thank you."

"Tonight?" I asked.

"Let me make it through today first."

"In case your day gets busy, just remember that I love you, Vee Hubbard."

Her cheeks rose. "I don't know about tonight. I do know I don't want to be alone." She laid her petite hand on my forearm. "I don't know what I'd have done these last few days without you."

"Your vibrator would have had a workout."

She shook her head. "There's more to life than sex."

I lifted my eyebrows. "Really?"

Vee snickered. "I love you. Stay safe during practice."

"I'm more concerned about the locker room." We came to a stop in front of the main building.

"Good luck." She grabbed her leather satchel and opened the door. "We've got this." The door slammed shut.

For a moment, I watched Vee's round ass and her long hair sway as she confidently made her way to the glass doors and disappeared inside. I could handle whatever came my way, and while I wanted to wrap Vee in Bubble Wrap, I had faith that she could manage whatever came her way.

After parking my truck, I grabbed my duffel bag and headed inside toward the locker room. Greetings and nods came from other players. It wasn't until I was putting on my shoulder pads that Troy, Jamir, and Dijon came to my locker. They were already dressed for practice.

"So?" Troy asked as he took a seat on the bench.

"So," I replied, "you're getting reps today."

"Last I heard, I'm not getting playing time until after the bye. But it's good to be practicing again."

JD joined our group. "Talk to us, Fin."

I stared around at all four sets of eyes. "Okay, what do you want to talk about?"

JD slapped my shoulder pad. "Teammates...yeah,

we need to trust one another." He looked to the other men. "Ain't that right?"

"Sure is," Jamir said. "Like, I'm your running back. I need to know I can count on you."

"Has that been an issue?"

JD lowered his voice. "Just tell us if the rumors are true." When I didn't answer, he pulled out his phone. On the screen was the picture of me with the Cincinnati Reds cap. "Was this you on your way up to Ms. Maeve's place?"

"Yeah, it's me. Vee and I go way back. She just unexpectedly and tragically lost her father."

JD whistled. "Oh, it's Vee not Maeve."

Troy's smile broadened. "We were right about a woman."

"Our Fin," Dijon said, "didn't settle for a Coopers groupie. Fuck no, he's banging the owner's daughter."

"Fuck that," JD said. "The owner."

I turned, my jaw set and my body ready to lash out. My tenor dropped. I twisted the front of Dijon's practice jersey with my fist and brought our faces close together. "Never fucking say anything like that about Vee—ever," I growled. "She's a lady, not someone who gets *banged*."

Dijon leaned away and lifted his hands in surrender. "You're right, Fin. Sorry." He looked around. We had the attention of most of the locker room. "Ms. Maeve is cool."

Heads nodded.

"Listen," JD said, "be good to her, or we, your team-mates, will have to kick your ass."

I released Dijon's jersey. "Just so we're clear. I can kick all your asses."

The men around me laughed.

My volume rose. "I can and I will." A smile cracked my angry expression. "As long as you're all kind enough to take your turn and let this old man rest in between."

Troy stood and patted my shoulder. "Seriously, Fin. Tell her we believe in her."

"Graham," came from a booming voice we all recognized.

"Tilson," Dijon whispered.

"Over here," I yelled.

"Get in my office. Everyone else, get your asses out on the practice field. We have a game to win Sunday."

CHAPTER 18

Vee

"Oh, Vee," Jen said, her eyes growing wide. "What happened to you? Are you all right?"

I gingerly touched my cheek. "Would you believe I ran into a wall?"

"No." She stood and walked toward me.

A feigned smile spread across my lips. "I was in a car accident last night."

She gasped. "First Mr. Hubbard and then you."

I hadn't thought of it that way. "It was nothing. I drove my car off the road near my dad's house. Those country roads have deep ravines. I was going slow. There were reporters." I shook my head. "The airbags deployed. I think it was the one from the steering wheel that gave me the shiner. Now that I'm thinking about it, they took my car to the Mercedes dealership off Highway 25 downtown. Could you call them to find out how long it will take for them to fix it? And if it's not today, I'd like to get a rental."

Fin's advice about security wasn't bad advice. However, I was too independent to have a bodyguard around all the time. That seemed suffocating.

"Sure. Also, Mrs. Marsh would like to talk to you when you have a moment."

My aunt.

"I have an important call to make. After that, I'll contact Aunt Rachel."

"Coffee?" she asked.

"Please."

Esquire Tricia Loften had an excellent résumé. She graduated top of her law class from the University of Chicago and clerked for Justice Meredith Stinwell, a respected federal judge in the Eastern District of Kentucky, for two years post-graduation. Tricia then declined an offer to enter one of the top law firms in Lexington to work for the federal public defender's office. After three years in that role, Tricia accepted a position at the prestigious Davis and Barnes Law Firm in Frankfort, Kentucky. That acceptance was twenty years ago. Today, she was a partner at Davis and Barnes.

Using Cammy's name, I was connected to Esquire

Loften without much delay. "Thank you for taking my call, Esquire Loften."

"Ms. Hubbard, Cammy Wilcox let me know a little about your situation. She said she believes you should have legal representation that is focused on you, not the Coopers or your late father."

I sighed, put the phone on speaker, and laid it on my desk. "I appreciate Cammy's help. That's exactly why I'm calling."

"First, please call me Trish. May I call you Maeve?"

"Vee is good. Thank you, Trish." I flexed my fingers, feeling the ache that Fin said would be worse today.

"Very well. I'd like to hear more from you about what you're seeking and together we can decide if we're a good fit."

I leaned back against my leather chair. "As you're aware, my father, Reid Hubbard, died recently in an automobile accident."

"I am and I'm sorry. How are you doing?"

"Thank you." Her question threw me off, filling my eyes with moisture. The only other person to ask how I was doing was Fin. "I'm not sure how I'm doing. There hasn't been time to fully process what happened. It feels like I'm a snowball rolling downhill, faster and faster, collecting more snow as I go."

"Everyone processes their grief in their own way."

"I'll deal with that when I have time. Right now, I have concerns about various issues surrounding my father's death. First, his estate. My father had talked about changing his will. He had a new will drafted but never signed it. His last will and testament was signed over twenty years ago and leaves everything to me."

"You are his only child."

She hadn't asked a question, but I answered, "I am. He also left behind a wife."

"Not your mother?"

"No. His widow's name is Daphne Hubbard. They've been married for over twenty-two years."

"And she's not mentioned in your father's will."

"She's not. There's something else. Last night, a Kentucky state trooper and a detective came to my house. They said they were investigating my father's accident. The company who owns the truck that caused the accident is contesting the original findings. They're claiming it wasn't the truck driver's fault but my father's."

"Vee, I'm happy to represent you. I haven't seen any numbers, but I would assume your father's estate is valuable?"

"I haven't seen the numbers either," I confessed, "but from what I understand it is."

"It isn't uncommon that wealthy individuals and businesses are sued, if they think there could be a payday. Let me look into this."

"Thank you," I said gratefully. "I'm overwhelmed."

"While I'd like to meet in person, we don't have to

wait for that. Once I receive a retainer, I will officially be your personal attorney."

"Let's get that done."

My mind was scrambled with too many fires.

Sipping coffee and weeding through my emails, I remembered the picture the detective showed me the night before. The small intricate pillbox was exactly like one I'd had for years. I couldn't understand how or why my pillbox would be in Dad's car.

The pillbox wasn't unique. Maybe we both had the same one.

I looked in my leather bag again, as if I could have missed the pillbox last night. It hadn't miraculously appeared. Getting up, I went to my attached bathroom and checked the vanity drawers as well as the medicine cabinet.

The more I thought about it, the less I could recall having the pillbox. Usually, every spring I would swap out the old Benadryl for new. It was now the middle of October, and my memory was blank.

A knock at my office door garnered my attention seconds before Jen popped her head inside. "Coach Pratt is here."

"Send him in." I walked back to my desk.

Drew Pratt came through the doorway wearing a Coopers workout suit. The jacket was unzipped, showing a black Dri-FIT shirt beneath.

"Hey, Vee." He furrowed his brow. "What happened to you?"

"Car accident. I ran off the road and the airbags won." I grimaced as I took a seat. "Drew, what can I do for you?"

"Practice started, and you're not out there. I wondered if you would be at any of the practices today or in the future." He grinned. "We're used to you being there."

Suddenly, the subject of Fin and I having a relationship came to me. "Um, how are things with the players?"

"The players are good." He tilted his head. "Are you asking about a particular player?"

"Drew, if you don't know, Fin—"

He lifted his hand. "Vee, it's none of my concern. I'm not judging. I'm in no position nor is anyone on the team in a position to tell you what to do with your private life."

"You know about us."

He nodded. "Tilson called Graham in this morning, and he talked to all the coaches. He said there's a history between you and him. He took full responsibility for pursuing you upon his arrival to Lexington."

Accountability.

My grin curled. "It's mutual, Drew. Fin and I do have a history. I don't want this to affect his play for the Coopers. It shouldn't. I didn't negotiate his contract;

Dad and Royce did that. I don't coach him. You, Tilson, and Garcia do that. I don't care for the timing of people finding out, but it is what it is. During this time of loss, I'm happy to have Fin to help me."

He nodded. "Calmer heads prevailed. Tilson checked Graham's contract. This situation isn't specifically addressed in the contract. No breach."

"That's good to hear. I'm glad it's out in the open."

"Practice?" When I didn't reply, he said, "The players respect you, Vee. That's not going to change because of who you're seeing in your personal time."

"It's...I can't do what I did and also do Dad's job." I didn't even really know what Dad's job entailed.

Drew nodded. "Just so you know, you're welcome. The afternoon practice session will begin at 1:30 p.m."

"Thank you for checking on me."

He turned to leave and then turned back. "I saw the notice for Reid's service."

"We want to keep it small, but Daphne and I agreed that the people here at Maker's Mark are family: coaches, players, and everyone who keeps the organization going. The service won't be open to the public."

Jen knocked on the doorframe. "I'm sorry to interrupt. Mrs. Marsh is here."

CHAPTER 19

Fin

With my helmet in hand, I jogged out of the football center to the practice field. The afternoon sun had warmed the earlier crisp autumn air. Around the field, trees were giving up their green in favor of yellows and oranges. Coopers' colors. The leaves were either cheering for our team or honoring Reid Hubbard.

My heart squeezed in my chest at the unexpected sight of the woman on the sideline. Vee had her trusty notebook against her breasts and was talking with Coach Pratt. The long brown hair with golden highlights that had been down this morning was now secured near the nape of her neck. With her back turned toward the end zone, she didn't see me.

Moments like these when I could watch Vee

without her knowledge invigorated me. That made me sound like a voyeur. I didn't see it that way. No, I thought of my fascination as more of that of an art aficionado. Vee was a masterpiece, the pièce de résistance of the female variety. I'd spent too many years trying to get over her. Her worth was that of a priceless treasure. I happened to be someone who appreciated viewing the treasure that she was in her truest form.

Drew said something that made Vee turn. Even with her sunglasses, I could feel her focus on me as a smile curled her lips. There wasn't a wave or even a nod, yet I knew she'd just seen me.

She turned back to Drew.

Of course, the coaches saw the social media. It was viral. Anyone with any social media account had probably seen it. When Tilson called me to his office, I was met by the entire coaching staff. Something Vee said to me during our argument came back. She said she took me for someone who took personal accountability. In that moment, she was correct that I was blaming her for what happened long ago. Walking in Tilson's office, I was the man she thought I should be. I told them the truth. Vee and I had a history, and I actively pursued her once I was signed onto the Coopers.

It felt good to come clean.

Tilson informed me that he couldn't find a breach of contract. I didn't tell him Jackson, my agent, had already scoured the contract. I simply said thank you.

Our coaches spent yesterday dissecting the Raiders' playbook and going over films from their last five games. The Raiders had a record of 4 and 1. Their only loss went to the Seahawks in a nail-biting 9–6 game that ended with a Seahawks' field goal. The Raiders' defense had only given up twenty-two points all season, and average of 4.4 a game. They were one of the top-rated defenses in the NFL.

That meant that our offense needed to overcome their defense.

Whistles sounded around the practice field. The play calling began.

Draw play.

Play action.

Screen play.

Quarterback draw.

The Coopers' practice defense squad was on the field simulating our future opponents. They didn't know our play calls and we didn't know theirs. It was the best way to replicate a true defense.

I lined up under center with my receivers in split-back formation. The defense moved from the 4–4 defense into 5–2. The play I was told to call wouldn't work; their loaded defense was designed to stop the run and left the backfield vulnerable to a pass.

I called an audible, letting the offense know that we had an RPO. "Gun king trips right tear 52 sway all go special X-shallow cross H-wide. Kill. Kill." I danced back five yards as my running backs took off, Dijon going post and Treshawn going corner.

The offensive line was holding the linemen and giving me time to read my reps.

Using man coverage, the defensive corners and safeties had both running backs covered. Ramel Patel, our wide receiver, was open. My arm went back and then forward as I was hit from the blind side.

My ass was on the ground; the ball was out. The defense recovered it.

Turnover.

"Fuck."

"Hey, Fin," Pickett, the defensive end who sent me flying, said as he offered me his hand.

Taking it, I stood. "You're not going to be on the practice squad for long if you keep knocking the shit out of me. Brown will make you active."

Pickett scoffed. "I'm learning your tells."

"Fuck that. I don't have tells."

"You do, man." He winked and jogged away.

"Graham," Pratt yelled. "Do it again. And Young, don't let the defense slip through."

The afternoon progressed. While I only had one interception and the one turnover, I was knocked on my ass plenty of times. Tonight, I'd be the one who needed the salt bath.

Each time I checked the sidelines, Vee was watching and taking notes. As I sat on the bench, my eyes went between watching her and watching Troy Dennison take reps. That was when I noticed Pickett standing farther down the field and made my way over to him. "What are they?"

His lips quirked. "I have an advantage of watching you every day. Other defensive ends don't have that."

"Yeah, but they've got film. If you're seeing something, I want to know what you see."

"You read your reps left to right. Most QBs do. You blink your eyes when you find your target. It's fast, man, real fast. Then you act like you're going to throw the opposite direction. You faked right. I know that means you're throwing left. You had Patel in your sights."

"Shit." I exhaled. "You're fucking with my head."

"No, Fin. I'm good."

"Would you be able to see that on film?"

Pickett shrugged. "If I watched the same QB enough."

"Twelve years in the league and six in college. No one, no coach, no player has told me that. And the thing is you're right."

"What you're doing is working."

I shook my head. "I need to work on that." A smile spread across my lips. "Thank you."

"Sure thing. I'll knock you on your ass a hundred more times. Maybe I'll get Coach Brown's attention."

"You should already have it."

"Graham," Coach Garcia called. "You're in."

I reached for my helmet and trotted onto the field. "You look good," I said to Troy as we passed on the field.

"Feels good to be back out here."

My smile quirked. "I'm ready for the front-row seat."

"We know the Raiders' defense is fucking tough," Coach Pratt said. "They're fast and they're mean. Graham, your time in the pocket needs to get faster. Lewis, Patel, and Downing, run those routes and get seconds off your time. O line, watch the gaps, don't let the tackles in. Now, let me see you work on that. We'll start with play-action in I formation." He held up his old-time stopwatch. "I'm timing you."

Every muscle in my body ached as I stood under the hot shower spray in the locker room shower. Coach Pratt and Coach Garcia's calls were running laps through my brain. Faster. Faster. Faster. Tomorrow we'd concentrate on third-down situations. Friday would be red zone and speed. Saturday, in Las Vegas, we would put it all together into a package that would hopefully result in a Sunday victory. NFL rules stated that teams traveling by air must be in the host city no less than eighteen hours before kickoff.

Tilson announced the team plane was leaving early Saturday morning. We'd be ahead of the NFL schedule while having time to practice in Vegas and adjust to the time change. After drying off, I wrapped my towel around my waist and made my way into the locker room. Many of the players were already gone. Troy was at his locker, not far from mine.

"How did it feel?" I asked.

"Great."

"You looked good."

He turned, his eyes focused on my chest. "Jesus, you got beat up out there."

Smiling, I looked down at the red contusion on my chest. "Just a lead-up for Sunday."

"No, I was watching. You were moving faster. Ramel, Dijon, JD, were really booking it. You keep that up and the Raiders' defense won't stop you."

I lifted my right arm and rotated my shoulder. "I hope I can get out of bed in the morning."

Troy laughed. "When do you think the reporters will back off from the gate?"

"Hopefully soon."

"I was talking to Ms. Maeve. She took off her sunglasses..." His eyes were drilling into mine.

"She was in a car accident last night."

"No shit. I didn't say anything, but it bothered me, seeing her with that shiner."

"Airbags deployed and seat belt...she's sore but safe."

"Maybe you two can commiserate together."

It was my turn to grin. "That's the plan."

"Tomorrow," Troy said as he picked up his bag and walked away.

After I was dressed, I checked my phone. I had one text message from Vee.

"JEN WAS ABLE TO GET ME A RENTAL CAR. I'LL SEE YOU AT HOME."

THE HOME PART of the text made me smile. The rental car, I wasn't as thrilled about. We'd have something to discuss while soaking in bath salts.

CHAPTER 20

Vee

Maker's Mark was beginning to clear out for the evening as I left my office. Heading toward the front doors, I changed my mind and turned in another direction. There was a longing or ache within me, one that had been growing throughout the day. Being back out on the sidelines made me think about Dad. He'd wanted me to understand the entire football business and operations. I wanted to be out there. When I was, I felt somehow closer to him.

Things had been so busy since that horrible morning, I wanted to be closer to him, if only for a few minutes. I turned toward the executive offices. I hadn't stepped foot in his office since the morning of the accident. Even though I know Bre and her staff were present earlier in the day, the front office was dark. Scanning the larger space with numerous desks, I had a new appreciation for the complexity of the CEO position.

The weight that revelation placed on my shoulders was staggering.

Looking around, I noticed that the doors to Dad's office were closed; however, golden light spilled out under the wooden barriers.

Did someone leave the light on?

I attempted to turn the knob, but it remained in place. The doors were locked. I was about to walk away when I heard what I thought was a woman crying.

Is someone in his office?

"Aunt Rachel?" I called. She was Dad's sister and even though she'd been strong this morning when we spoke, maybe she was feeling the way I was. "Aunt Rachel."

There was no answer.

The crying stopped.

"Aunt Rachel."

I knocked on the door. "It's Vee. Let me in." I waited. "I'm not leaving."

Finally, I heard the sound of the locking mechanism disengaging. Slowly, one of the doors opened inward. I stared in shock at the woman inside. "Bre?"

Dad's assistant's gaze met mine, her eyes red and puffy. "Um, Vee…"

It was then that I looked beyond her, stunned by the disarray within his private office and adjoining rooms. It hadn't been like this the morning of the accident. Things were haphazardly piled on Dad's desk. Drawers were open. His closet was opened. Slowly, I stepped forward and spun. Even drawers in the bathroom were opened. "What the hell is going on in here?"

"I-I thought everyone was gone."

My neck straightened as the small hairs on the back of my neck stood to attention. "Bre, what the hell are you doing with Dad's things?"

Bre wiped tears still flowing down her cheeks. "It occurred to me that soon you or someone else will take over this office."

I nodded.

"There are things...things that Reid wouldn't want..." She took a ragged breath and met my stare. "It's no one's business."

"The Coopers is my business."

"Fuck, Vee. It's not about the Coopers."

My eyes roamed around the room. Curiosity pulled me toward the mess on top of his desk. "What's all of this?"

Moving quickly, Bre blocked my path. "Really, Vee. It would be better if no one in the family knew about this. I mean, Reid...he wouldn't want that."

I shook my head, trying to make sense of what

didn't make sense. Then I saw the corner of a printed picture. Reaching around Bre, I pulled the photo from a pile of papers. My eyes opened wide at the sight of a selfie of Dad and Bre. She was on his lap in the chair behind this desk. They were both smiling.

My stomach dropped.

"You and Dad were…" I could hardly form the words. "You were having an affair?"

Bre's demeanor changed, sadness and grief morphing into defiance. She ripped the photo from my grasp. "It was more than an affair. That word sounds… dirty." She smirked. "Reid was a good man in an unhappy marriage."

"How long…?"

She squared her shoulders. "A couple of years."

"Years?" Her answer felt like a gut punch.

"Don't act so high and mighty. You're the last person to judge. We all know about you and Griffin Graham."

"Dad was married. Fin and I are both single. There's no comparison."

"Do you really want this information to get out too?" she asked, holding up the picture. "As if your affair with Mr. Graham isn't already harming the Coopers."

"We're in a relationship. That's not an affair."

"You want the world to remember Reid as an owner, CEO, and family man, or for this?"

I walked to the desk and began to rifle through the papers. My stomach twisted as I read intimate notes from Dad to Bre and others from her to him. I recognized his penmanship right away. My nose wrinkled as sour stomach acid made its way up my throat. Each one was signed with love or a heart.

My stomach twisted. "Dad was sixty-five. You're what...forty?"

"Forty-one." Her lips curled. "Your father was a powerful, amorous lover."

I shook my head. "Stop."

Bre took a deep breath.

"Did the two of you have plans?" I finally asked. "Or were you supposed to go on forever as the other woman?"

"We had plans." Bre stormed out the door.

I followed a step behind.

Bre opened the top drawer of her desk and pulled out a small robin's-egg-blue box—Tiffany's. Opening the hinged box, she took a large solitary diamond ring out and slid it onto the fourth finger of her left hand. "He wanted to marry me."

"He told you that?"

She looked longingly down at the ring. "We were both looking forward to the day I could wear this out in the open."

"How...how long ago did he give that to you?"

"Last year after the end of the season."

I didn't want to think about my dad as any kind of lover. I also didn't want to think of him as a cheater, but that timeline seemed long. "If he meant what he said, wouldn't his marriage be over by now?"

"Daphne." Bre's nostrils flared. "She was manipulating him."

"*She* was manipulating Dad," I repeated. "Or was he manipulating *you*?"

"No, don't say that. He wouldn't do that. We had plans. Reid was going to divorce Daphne. He was tired of her constant spending and whining. He wanted to be with a woman with more depth than a pothole."

Okay, that fit.

"And that woman was you?"

"Vee, I'm telling you the truth. Reid was going to file for divorce after the end of this season. We were supposed to go on an overseas trip where we'd marry and honeymoon." The tears were back, coating Bre's cheeks. "He loved me. I loved him."

I scrunched my nose. "Did he talk to Mr. Eads about a divorce?"

"Yes," she said defiantly. "We—our relationship— was the real reason Reid hadn't signed the new will. He didn't want to leave anything to her. He wanted it to go to me."

I blinked repeatedly, as if it would make everything clear. "To you?"

"Not everything. He promised ten percent."

My eyes opened wider. That was the amount he'd told me was for Daphne.

She sweetened her tone. "He wasn't going to leave you or the Marshes out. Reid would never do that."

This was unexpected, too much, more than I wanted to handle at the moment. I straightened my neck. "You're right, Bre."

"I am?"

"Yes." I motioned toward the open doors to Dad's office. "Clean it out." My tone became colder, nearing freezing. "All of it. Everything and anything that incriminates you or Dad. Take it home. Burn it. I don't care what you do with it. I want it all gone by tomorrow."

"I-I" —she was crying again— "I can't believe he's really gone."

My sympathy was reserved for those people who deserved it. While I didn't always consider Daphne as a part of that group, I never thought of Bre Stanton in that way.

"Please don't attend the service next Tuesday."

"What?" She opened her eyes. "I have to be there. I must get the chance to tell him goodbye."

"You're uninvited," I said as I turned and left Bre alone with her own mess.

It wasn't until I was in the rental car that I screamed. No words, only a bloodcurdling scream coming from deep in my chest. I grimaced as I pounded the steering wheel with the butt of my hands. My throat was raw as I spoke to no one. "Dad, what the actual fuck? What other secrets did you have? What other bombshells are going to surface?"

Turning on the car, I connected my telephone and adjusted the seat and mirrors. The evening sky was beginning to darken. Crimsons and purples erupted like an old lava lamp over the horizon as I made my way out of the football center's parking lot. The Coopers' security guard was still in place.

"Good night, Ms. Hubbard."

"Good night." I rolled up the window, observing that there were fewer news vans and reporters than there had been this morning.

I called Aunt Rachel.

She answered on the third ring. "Vee, is everything okay?"

A scoff came from my lips. "No, but that's not why I'm calling." Earlier today we discussed traveling to Las Vegas. "I've decided we can take the Gulfstream to Las Vegas on Saturday morning."

"Oh, honey. Darin and I talked about it. We planned to take it on Friday just like Reid had planned. It is Vegas after all. We thought we deserved some fun."

"The family plane is not flying twice. I have too much to do here to leave on Friday." I would think she did too. "If you and Uncle Darin want to go on Friday, book a commercial flight. The Hubbard plane is flying

Saturday morning." I didn't wait for a response as I disconnected the call.

I spoke to the car. "Call Tony Witkoff." Tony was the Coopers' head pilot.

"Calling Tony Witkoff," the car said.

"Ms. Hubbard," Tony said upon answering. "What can I do for you?"

"I'm calling to let you know I've decided to fly to Las Vegas on Saturday morning. I can be at the airport by nine. From what Coach Tilson told me, that will be around the time the team is leaving."

"I spoke to Robert" —another pilot— "and he said the team will be leaving at ten."

"That will work. We'll get there first."

"Ms. Hubbard?"

"Yes?" I answered.

"Have you spoken to Mr. or Mrs. Marsh? They told me we were leaving on Friday."

"The Hubbard plane is leaving on Saturday. If Mr. and Mrs. Marsh wish to travel earlier, they are welcome to book another flight."

"Yes, ma'am."

"I'll see you Saturday," I said. "Goodbye." I disconnected the call.

The icon for a text message appeared on the screen. "Read text message."

. . .

"TEXT MESSAGE FROM FIN. WHERE ARE YOU? IF YOU ARE IN ANOTHER SITUATION THAT WOULD HAVE BEEN REMEDIED WITH SECURITY, ONCE YOU'RE HOME SAFE, I'M REDDENING YOUR SEXY ASS."

"OH," I said with a giggle. "Sorry, car. You're a rental, and you probably shouldn't have read that.

At the stoplight, I sent a quick text.

"SECURITY COULDN'T HAVE MADE A DIFFERENCE. YOU'RE BEING BOSSY AGAIN. ALMOST HOME."

CHAPTER 21

Fin

Ethan arranged for me to use a parking space in the lower-level garage at the Vine. The owners were out of town, snowbirds who had already flown Kentucky for the beaches of Florida. This new benefit allowed me entry up to the seventh floor without the hassle of baseball caps or disguises. My thighs ached as I stepped down from my truck. I didn't know what color or model rental car Vee had, but I was sad to see her parking space still empty.

Thankfully, I was able to go straight from my truck up to the seventh floor. The beeping of the security system confirmed that Vee wasn't here. I turned it off.

A smile tugged at my lips as I looked around. I had lived in many cities, moved from apartments to houses and to condominiums. In LA, I discovered the ease of renting—everything. As I prepared to move to Lexington, I followed that pattern. JD recommended the apartment complex, and a few phone calls later, I had a fully decorated place to sleep. Everything from the furniture to wall art, kitchenware to towels and sheets were waiting for me.

That was convenient, but it wasn't personal. Even after a year in LA, the apartment felt as if I was living in someone else's place. My new place was the same. Vee's condo reflected her personality. The modern, classy style was welcoming and light. Despite the darkening sky, the golden glow of lights from street level filled the living space with a Thomas Kinkade warm radiance.

I hit the lights and contemplated starting a fire in the fireplace.

Everything looked as it had been when we left in the morning, including the dishes in the sink. Throwing my duffel bag on the bed in the bedroom, I went to the kitchen to remedy the dirty dishes and think about dinner.

Part of me wanted to collapse, but the practical part of me was afraid that if I gave in to my aching body and sat down on the sofa, I wouldn't get back up. Opening the dishwasher, I arranged our coffee cups, plates, and a frying pan.

The ring of the doorbell echoed throughout the condo. Vee wouldn't use the doorbell. I was prepared for another encounter with Kentucky's finest. Instead, the sweet scent of roses assaulted my senses. The large bouquet of flowers obscured the delivery person's face, allowing me to see tan pants and nice leather loafers—expensive for a delivery person.

The flowers moved and I came face-to-face with a man about my age, average build, not too muscular, not overweight, with blue eyes.

"Who the fuck are you?" he said.

"Um, is this a delivery?"

The man leaned one direction and the other as if trying to look into the condo. "Is Vee here?"

I lifted my arm to the doorjamb, flexing my bicep, and narrowed my eyes. "How did you get up here?"

"I told the guard at the elevator I lived here."

"You don't live here."

He took a step back. "Fuck, you're Graham, from the Coopers."

"And you are...?"

His facial features contorted. "No fucking way. Are you living here with Vee?"

I could blame it on the hard workouts today, but my brain was obviously processing at a slower than normal rate. A slow smile curled my lips. "Preston Clark, of the horse Clarks."

"Thoroughbred. Is Vee here?"

"No." I inhaled, deducing that the roses were masking the scent of manure.

Clark thrust the flowers toward me. "Give these to..." He pulled them back. "Fuck no. Forget it."

"What is this?" Vee's voice came from the direction of the elevator.

Clark and I both turned.

"Honey," I called with as sticky sweet of a voice as I could muster. "You have a visitor."

Clark turned his attention to Vee. "What the fuck happened? Why do you have a black eye?"

Vee's fingers went to her cheek. "I was in a minor accident."

Clark's jaw clenched. "I've called and you haven't answered or returned my calls."

"I'm a little busy, Preston. My father just passed away."

"I know. I'm sorry. I was worried." He pushed the flowers forward. "I brought these for you. I thought... well, I didn't want you to be alone."

"She's not," I interjected.

Vee shook her head and gave me a side eye. "That's very sweet of you." She stood still, not taking the flowers. "I'm not alone. I am tired, and I want to end this conversation."

"Is *he*" —he jutted his chin toward me— "living here?"

We answered simultaneously.

"Yes," I replied.

"That's none of your business," Vee said and turned toward me, her lips pursed and green eyes wide.

I stepped forward, forcing Clark to back up a step or two. His retreat allowed Vee space to enter the condo. "Thanks for stopping by," I said with a feigned smile. "We'll have to do this again sometime."

Clark set his jaw and stared at me.

I stared back, losing the fake grin as Vee walked into the condo. If this guy wanted to go a round or two, while I was sore, I was confident I could wipe the floor with him. "I think it's time for you to leave."

The vase shattered as Clark dropped the roses at my feet, before turning and walking toward the elevator.

"What happened?" Vee asked, her hand on my back as she and I stared down at the shards of glass and tangled long-stemmed roses. "What an ass." She bent down.

I pulled her back up. "Stop. I'll get it. I don't want you to cut yourself."

"Okay. Let me get a broom and dustpan."

Crouching down, my thighs yelled as I began gathering the roses. "Ouch." I looked down at the drop of blood on my finger. "Damn thorns."

Vee came back with the kitchen trash container. "Put them in here."

"Don't you want to keep them?"

She shook her head.

"That guy has anger issues," I said. "I'm glad you're not with him." A terrible thought came to me, causing me to stop the cleanup and turn to Vee. "Tell me the truth. Did he ever hurt you?" I was ready to run down the stairs and find him in the lobby or out on the street.

"No." She sighed. "He's not like that. Part of the reason I broke things off with Preston was that he asked me to move in with him. I didn't want to. He asked if he could move in here." Vee spoke as she carefully picked up flowers, and I gathered the larger pieces of glass. "I told him that I wasn't ready for that." She nudged me with her shoulder. "You shouldn't have said you're living here."

"Well, damn. I didn't know that part of your history, and let's face it. Currently, I'm living here."

"You still have your own place."

I dropped the last large piece of glass in the trash can and leaned closer. Bringing my lips to hers, I smiled. "I do."

We stood.

I reached for the broom. "I can get the rest."

After the hallway floor was clean, I brought the broom, dustpan, and trash can back into the condominium and closed and locked the door. Vee was leaning against the kitchen counter watching me.

Setting the items down, I went to her. Caging her to the counter with one of my arms, I cupped her sore cheek with my other hand.

She inclined her face and sighed.

Leaning forward, I pressed my hips against hers. "You were gorgeous out on the sideline. I was surprised to see you."

Vee splayed her fingers over my chest. "Are you sore? You kept getting knocked down."

Reaching for her hand, I gently kissed her tender knuckles. "We may have to share the bath salts tonight."

Her cheeks rose as she smiled. "I've had a crazy day."

"How about I open the wine we started last night and call downstairs for dinner? Ethan or Jacob can bring it up and we can relax."

Vee furrowed her brow and tugged on her bottom lip with her teeth. "How did Preston get up here? I never gave him a keycard like you have."

"He said he told the security guard on the first floor he lives here."

She pressed her lips together. "We need to let security know. Anyone could do that."

"Speaking of security...?"

Her emerald eyes gleamed.

CHAPTER 22

Vee

"Fin, I've had a day. There's security at Maker's Mark. Uncle Darin arranged for extra security in Las Vegas. I have you here. I think I'm good." I brushed my lips over his. "The reason I'm late isn't about security or the lack thereof."

He took a step back and walked to the other counter. I scanned the definition of his biceps from beneath the sleeves of his shirt as he pulled two clean wine glasses from the rack, uncorked last night's bottle, and filled each globe with the semi-sweet red liquid. As he turned, his blue eyes were focused on me. "Here." His smile grew as he handed me a glass. "You're now in the let-yourself-relax-and-leave-everything-to-Fin world."

A long hum left my lips. "I like the sound of that."

"Do you want to talk about your day?"

I took a hearty sip of my wine. "I don't know." Kicking off my shoes, I walked barefoot into the living room to the tall windows. The bubbling lava lamp at the horizon was gone. The sky above was a black dome, the stars masked by the city lights. Closing my eyes, I pictured Bre, the pictures, and the notes.

Opening my eyes, I saw Fin's reflection in the windowpane as he came up behind me and wrapped an arm around me. Exhaling, I leaned my head back against his solid chest. "I learned something today."

"About...?"

"Something I wish I didn't know."

He tugged me closer and kissed the top of my head. "Would this *something* be about the Coopers, your accident, or Reid?"

It was the first time I'd heard Fin refer to my dad by his first name. While I didn't mind, it also made me sad that these two men would never have the chance to truly know one another. Blinking, I fought a new round of tears. "He was the best father."

"You didn't learn that today."

I took another sip of the wine and spun in Fin's embrace. Looking up, I swallowed my emotion. "If I tell you something, something I never imagined, I can trust you, right? You won't say anything about it to anyone."

"Vee, you can trust me with your gorgeous body,

your deepest secrets, your greatest ambitions, your utmost fears. I want every part of you."

Sighing, I tipped my forehead against his chest. It was easier to say the words if I wasn't looking into Fin's sapphire-blue orbs. In the car, I'd decided to keep Dad's secret forever. Each mile, the burden grew. I didn't want the world to know, but I wanted to share the heavy weight with someone I could trust. Just like the way I planned to tell Dad about Fin and me, I chose to blurt it out. "Dad was having an affair."

"Shit. What?" Fin asked as he pulled my chin upward.

"Yeah." I nodded. "I went to his office after work. I don't know what drew me there. He was the one who encouraged me to learn more about football opera-tions. I wasn't sure I'd return to the sideline." I shook my head. "I'm so overwhelmed with the idea of CEO. But Drew came to find me after the morning practice and said I was still welcome."

"As if he could stop you."

"No, I don't think he meant it like that. He said you'd talked to the coaches."

Fin nodded and released my chin. "Come over to the couch. Let's sit."

I set my glass on the oval glass table and settled close to Fin. His arm again wrapped around me, and I inhaled his sandalwood scent. "I think Drew came to me to let me know that the players and coaches knew about the two of us and it didn't matter."

"Good."

"I had a million things to do, but I spent the afternoon on the sidelines. The play calling is getting easier to understand." That reminded me. "Oh, that practice defensive end is fast."

"Pickett. He's fast, smart, observant, and painful."

My lower lip pushed forward. "The reason for the bath salts?"

"Yeah. Keep talking. You went to your dad's office..."

"As I was leaving work," I went on, "I was thinking about him. I guess I thought I'd feel closer to him in his office. Anyway, when I got there, the central office was dark. There was a light coming from underneath Dad's office doors and when I tried to enter, they were locked. I started to walk away, and then I heard crying. It was a woman, so I assumed it was my aunt. You know, maybe she was feeling the same way I was. I knocked and called out to her."

"It wasn't your aunt," Fin said.

"No. It was Dad's assistant." I hesitated to say her name. "The office was a wreck. Things pulled from drawers...She tried to stop me from seeing anything, but I saw a picture—a physical picture. Of the two of them, smiling. She was on Dad's lap."

Fin lifted his eyebrows. "Oh shit."

"She proceeded to tell me that the affair had been going on for years. She showed me an engagement ring and told me as soon as Dad and Daphne divorced, he planned to elope with Bre to Europe—actually, she just said overseas."

"Do you believe her?"

"She had the receipts. There were little notes and letters from Dad to her and vice versa. I read more than I should have."

"I'm sorry, Vee. That shouldn't take away from the fact he was a great father."

"I know. It's just..." We intertwined our fingers. "Oh, she also said that she's the reason Dad hadn't signed the new will. He didn't plan to leave anything to Daphne but to Bre instead."

"Bre Stanton?"

I craned my neck to see his face. "You know her?"

Fin shook his head. "Not really. She was part of the communication chain during my first interactions with the Coopers."

"That's why I'm upset. Aunt Rachel had her at a meeting the other day. If anyone knows Dad's job, it's Bre. Now I want her gone."

"Because you're loyal to Daphne?"

"No," I answered too fast. "It feels...wrong."

"You know, if you decide to appoint yourself as CEO, you have the support of the players." His grin reappeared. "After I confessed to the others on the team about us, they told me to treat you right or they'd kick my ass."

I snickered. "Is that why Pickett kept knocking you down?"

"Have I not treated you right?"

Reaching up, I palmed his cheek, and stretching my neck, I brought my lips to his. "We should both be on probation for a while, but so far, I'd give you a passing grade."

"Oh, that sounds like a glowing assessment."

I shook my head. "If anything, you've treated me too well. When I'm here with you, I can almost forget the rest of the world, no matter how horrible it is."

"That's all part of the Fin's-in-control bubble we're creating. I'll look up the Vine's menu and we can order dinner." Again, he kissed the top of my head. "Getting beat up today made me hungry." Releasing my hand and easing his arm out from behind me, Fin stood.

"Wait." I reached for his hand. "What about my dad and Bre?"

"I don't know what to say. I'm against cheating. It's not something I would do."

I narrowed my gaze, remembering the pictures of him at Tennessee.

"I know what you're thinking," he said with a sexy grin. "To quote a nostalgic TV show, 'we were on a break.'"

I raised my eyebrows in question. "Fourteen years?"

"I can apologize to you for the rest of our lives, but in my mind, we were broken up."

Pressing my lips together, I nodded. "I'm sorry too. If I had told you who my dad was, the two of you would have had a chance to know one another."

Fin squeezed my hand. "You know on Wednesdays—today—there's no talk about the last game. Doesn't matter if it's a win or a loss. It's over. In the past. Our focus is on the next game and the next opponent. You and I both made mistakes. That was the discussion for Monday. Now, we've moved on to our future."

Grinning, I nodded.

We released each other's hand.

Fin started to walk toward the kitchen and stopped. His forehead furrowed. "Do you think Daphne knew?"

I let out a long sigh. "I don't know. If she did, I actually feel sorry for her. I think it's a secret better left buried."

"If you would fire Bre, could the secret come out?"

Reaching for my temples, I leaned back against the sofa. "I'm not sure screwing my late father is a justified reason for dismissal." My eyes opened wide. "However, Kentucky is an 'at-will' state, meaning I could fire her or anyone else for no reason."

"She could still fight it, and then your dad's secret would become public."

"One thing doesn't add up. Mr. Eads, Dad's attorney, specifically mentioned that Dad wanted Daphne to have more. And Bre said Mr. Eads knew of Dad's plans to divorce." I shook my head. "Right now, it's too much to think about." I reached for my wine. "I'm not sure I can work side by side with her day after day." I took another drink. "You don't need to look up the menu. I have it taped inside a cupboard in the kitchen." I shrugged. "It's convenient, and I'm not always in the mood to cook, especially for one." My forehead furrowed. "If Dad had this secret, are there more?"

Fin shook his head to my question. Honestly, neither one of us had the answer.

"Let's check out the menu," he said. "You've thought too much about the world outside our bubble. It's time for me to distract you."

"I really like the way that sounds."

CHAPTER 23

Vee

Gripping the railing, I stopped and looked up the stairs leading up to the family's Gulfstream. If I gave into my emotions, I would sit on the bottom step and cry. Even acknowledging my feelings was a slippery slope, one that I couldn't afford to slide down.

The last five days seemed to go on and on forever. And yet it also seemed like our flight to Green Bay was only a few days ago—my last flight with Dad. He and Daphne arrived just before takeoff. I could picture their smiles and Dad's sparkling green stare.

A black car pulled up onto the tarmac.

Turning, I waited to see who would emerge.

My mouth opened in surprise as Daphne and Grant appeared. "Daphne?"

The autumn breeze blew her long blond hair around her face as they both came toward me. Grant's business casual was on point with well-tailored pants, a white button-up shirt, and a camel sports jacket. Daphne portrayed the mourning widow in tight black slacks, and a long amber sweater with a wide belt. Their driver carried their overnight bags to the cargo hold of the plane.

Daphne reached out to Grant for support as she maneuvered her four-inch-heeled boots and large purse across the tarmac. I watched in disbelief as they smiled at one another.

They came to a stop. The concoction of cologne and perfume withstood the cooling breeze. Daphne was the first to speak. "You look surprised to see me, Vee."

"I didn't know you were coming."

"I almost didn't make it," she said. "Grant was sweet enough to let me know when the plane was leaving. I hadn't heard from you."

Clenching my teeth, I feigned a smile at my cousin. "You are so sweet, Grant."

His lips quirked. "I do my best."

"Let's get on board," I said. Inhaling, I made my way up the stairs. The wide legs of my brown slacks caught the breeze like sails. Thankfully, my boots only had two-inch heels, allowing me to steady myself as I stepped into the cabin.

"Are we all here?" I asked as I surveyed our passengers. Uncle Darin and Aunt Rachel were present, having decided to wait for the family plane. Leigh, Lip, and Hayden were seated in the aft at the four-person table. Greetings, albeit terse, were said all around as I made my way back to my cousins. "Mind if I join you?"

Leigh stood and wrapped me in a hug. My promise this morning to Fin and myself to stay unemotional was getting more difficult to keep. I quickly hugged her back.

"I'm glad you decided to join us." I pulled away and waved to Hayden and Lip. "Gang's all here."

Lip scooted over, giving me access to the fourth seat. Leigh leaned across the table. "Shit, Vee, do you have a bruise on your cheek?"

I tenderly palpated the sore. "I thought I did a decent job of covering it with makeup. It really is much better." With my cousins' eyes wide, I continued. "Tuesday night after I left Daphne's, I drove off the road. You know how deep those ravines are. The airbag deployed." I'd told the story enough times to recite it in my sleep.

"Susan," Daphne called to one of our hosts. "A rum and Diet Coke before takeoff, dear."

Lip nudged my shoulder.

"Oh," I whispered. "Did I eyeroll too loud?"

He smiled and kept his voice low. "I didn't realize Aunt Daphne was coming."

I lifted my eyebrows. "Yeah, I didn't get that memo either. Apparently, Grant was *sweet enough* to let her know when we were leaving."

"Sweet? That's a new description of my brother."

"Vee," Leigh said, "I'm glad you waited until this morning. I can't take off work as easily as all of you. I hate missing the away games." She smiled at her husband. "And leaving on Saturday, Hayden could come too."

"Your parents aren't as appreciative."

She shook her head. "Don't worry about them."

From my bag I removed the folder of papers that Bre had given me days ago. "I'm over my head."

Lip took the folder. "What is this? More play calls?"

"No," I said, keeping our conversation just between us. "It's an example of what Dad does...did. His assistant put it together."

Lip opened the folder. "From my perspective and those of us in brand and strategy, all of us flying to the game together is important. The Coopers are known as a family business. If Mom and Dad would have flown separately, it could send the message that there's dysfunction in the Coopers' executive offices."

Scoffing, I shook my head. "Dysfunction? Yeah, we don't want to let that get out."

"Seriously, Vee," Lip said. "I talked to my parents and shut down the idea of them traveling separately."

"So I have you to thank for their warm greetings."

"There's a lot that needs to be settled."

I pulled back the folder. "I've been so busy with my duties, I haven't had a chance to dive into this."

"Excuse me," Susan said.

We all turned our attention to her.

"First, we're all very sorry."

Pressing my lips together, I swallowed and nodded.

"The pilot is doing his final check. May I get anyone anything before we take off?"

Our flight would be approximately four and a half hours wheels up to wheels down. We gave Susan our drink orders. Unlike Daphne, the four of us chose to remain alcohol free, seeing as it was only nine in the morning—six in Vegas. Once we were in the air, I waffled between reading Bre's notes and conversing with my cousins. Despite all that was happening, we managed to keep our conversation light with few mentions of Dad or the Coopers.

It was after we'd eaten an early lunch that Leigh breached the subject of Fin. "I was surprised you two went public when you did. Is everything still good?"

I let out a long sigh. "It wasn't our choice to go public. Fin was spotted by a reporter in the elevator that goes up to the floor where I live. They made assumptions."

"Accurate assumptions," Hayden said with a grin.

"Assumptions, nonetheless," I replied. "At first, I hoped it would subside. When it didn't, we decided to take away the fuel of rumors. The story seemed to lose steam after we substantiated it."

"It's not as sensational," Lip said, "if it's a fact."

"Coopers' brand," I said, nudging his shoulder.

"We in branding got your order from the top to let the story ride." He quirked a smile. "Look at you making administrative decisions already."

I shook my head. "In case you were wondering, I won't be in the suite Sunday."

Hayden and Leigh nodded.

"On the sidelines?" Lip asked.

"Yeah. Honestly, it was what Dad encouraged. When I'm out there, I'm consumed with the plays, the game, and the players. It's surprisingly a retreat to be so absorbed in the action."

Leigh reached across the table and covered my hand. "Uncle Reid was very proud of what you were doing down there."

"I'm not doing anything. I'm watching and learning."

She shook her head. "To hear him talk about it, what you were doing was much more than that. You were constructing an important bridge between the Coopers on the field and the owner's suite."

I closed my eyes, fighting new tears. My nostrils flared as I blinked my eyes open and feigned a smile. "This is where I'm torn. Do I continue my role with stadium operations and marketing and building that bridge, or do I" —I patted the manila folder— "step into Dad's role?"

"Only you can decide that," Leigh replied.

After landing in Las Vegas, dry heat rushed inside the Gulfstream as the door opened.

"Vee," Uncle Darin said, "I arranged for the cars as normal. I didn't have a chance to talk to you…"

My smile strained. "At our last meeting, we discussed carrying on our roles. Thank you for arranging the cars, as something you've always done. Security?"

"That is arranged as well."

"After we check into our hotel…" Grant said. "We're staying at the Waldorf. I'm headed over to Allegiant Stadium in my capacity with communications."

"We can ride together," I offered. "Stadium operations are already in full gear."

The warm morning sun caused me to squint as I made my way down the stairs. Brown mountains in the distance and a bright blue sky above reminded me that we weren't in Lexington anymore. Keeping our seating the same, I rode to the hotel with Leigh, Hayden, and Lip. Aunt Rachel, Uncle Darin, Grant, and Daphne rode in the other car.

Even at the early hour—we'd gained three hours on our quest west—the city streets were congested and slow. I stared out of the car window at the giant signs, ones that would be lit up come nighttime. My thoughts were on stadium operations and the team's arrival. According to Tony, the team would only be an hour behind us.

Lip passed his phone to me. On the screen was a short video of all of us deboarding the plane. *Hubbards arrive in Las Vegas without Reid Hubbard* was on the bottom of the screen.

I shook my head. "I didn't see reporters."

He grinned. "This is why it was better for us all to be together."

Vee

The Coopers' equipment manager started the preparation for tomorrow's game over a week ago. He coordinated with the Raiders' stadium operations team for everything from game balls to our team's practice schedule. Our preliminary training staff were already at the practice facility, working with their counterparts in Las Vegas.

The NFL was a well-oiled machine. Not even the death of Reid Hubbard could bring it to a halt. Despite the giant void within me, the game would go on.

My hotel suite was large, too large. It was probably booked when I thought Preston might join me—back before. Now it was after. An unexpected knock on the door came as I was back in the bedroom unpacking. Apprehension prickled my skin as I peeked through the peephole revealing a woman close to my age with dark hair. Securing the safety lock, I opened the door a few inches. "Hello."

"Ms. Hubbard, I'm Virginia Athens from the Stephens Security Company. Mr. Marsh asked for me to be assigned to you this weekend."

This was news to me. I didn't recognize the company name and wasn't in the mood for company, especially that of a stranger. Plus, there was a questioning voice in my head warning me that she could be a reporter. "Ms. Athens, do you have ID?"

She proceeded to show me her identification as well as a plastic badge with the company's name.

"Can you wait just a minute?" I asked.

"Certainly."

Closing the door, I let out an exasperated breath. My temples pounded and the muscles in my neck tightened as I found my cellphone and called Uncle Darin.

"Vee," he said upon answering.

"What company did you hire for security?"

"Stephens. We've used them before. A woman named Athens has been assigned to you."

"She's here," I said. "I would have appreciated this information prior to her arrival."

His tone cooled. "I told you I arranged security."

"Not that we had personal...what is she, a bodyguard?"

"She has executive protection training. You want the top title; you should be ready to take what comes with it. The same news outlets that sent the reporters to Lexington know that we're here now."

"Dad didn't have this."

"He did on occasion. You didn't realize it because that's what these people do, fade into the background. Jesus Christ, Vee, you asked about security. I arranged it. Let her do her fucking job."

"Her fucking job." My voice slowed. "I want to do my fucking job. Don't assume I know details if you don't share them with me."

"Didn't Reid tell you not to micromanage?"

My jaw clenched. "I'm not having this conversation right now. I have a job to do." I tried to ignore my trembling hands as I disconnected the call.

Why did everything seem like a fight?

Gathering myself, I returned to the door and opened it wide. I gestured to Ms. Athens to come inside. "I'm sorry for the delay. Security arrangements were made without my input."

She smiled. "I assume you verified my information?"

"I did." I motioned to the bedroom. "I have a few more things to do here, and I'm headed to Allegiant Stadium. Um..." I shrugged. "You're welcome to sit out here." I looked around. "I'm new to this. How does this work?"

"I was told that you wanted to avoid the press."

"Very much."

"I'll accompany you whenever you're outside this room and until you leave Las Vegas tomorrow evening. Introduce me any way you want, an assistant, a coworker...I won't interfere with your job. My job is to keep others away from you."

Inhaling, I nodded, feeling unexpected relief. "Okay. We'll make this work." I feigned a smile. "I'll be ready in a few minutes."

"My company has a car ready for you and Mr. Marsh out a side door."

My thoughts went to my uncle. "Mr. Darin Marsh?"

"Mr. Grant Marsh." She lowered her eyebrows. "Did I read the instructions wrong? Aren't you riding together to the stadium."

"Oh yeah. We are. I'll hurry."

Grant was already in the car waiting when Virginia and I arrived. As the door opened, he pointedly looked down at his watch.

"You could have left without me," I offered.

"We're fine."

"Ms. Hubbard, I'm DeQuinta Jackson," the driver said.

"Nice to meet you." I settled in the back seat with Grant while Virginia took shotgun.

My phone buzzed in my bag. Pulling it out, I saw a text message from Fin. The team was officially in Las

Vegas. Their buses had police escort to the IMEG Training Center. "The team is here," I said to Grant.

He hummed. "Tilson reach out to you?"

Looking up, I met his gaze. "I have spies everywhere. I thought you knew that."

"Fuck, Vee," he growled under his breath. "It seems to me that the fact you're still involved with a player when the spotlight is on the Coopers shows your lack of commitment to the team."

My head was about to explode. "You know what shows lack of commitment?" I whispered, trying to keep our conversation from being overheard. "Wanting to leave a day early because it's Vegas and fun is deserved. It's only the sixth week of an eighteen-week season. My commitment is to the team. I'm beginning to wonder about others."

"My parents have worked their asses off for the Coopers, and for what?"

I shook my head. "I don't know the amount they've been paid, but I'll have the business office get me the figures on Monday. Everyone is well compensated. The rewards aren't so bad either, like flying to away games, accommodations, travel expenses. You are an important member of our family and executive team, Grant, but you're not indispensable."

Turning toward the front seat, I exhaled. My heart rate was thundering in my chest as I moved my head from side to side, trying to relieve the muscle strain.

My molars were about to explode from the pressure. This felt like it was a coordinated attack by father and son, and I for one wasn't going to put up with it.

While my cousin didn't reply verbally, the way his foot crossed over his knee bobbed and his fingers tapped on the door handle let me know he wasn't pleased.

That was good.

Neither was I.

The Raiders' home stadium was adjacent to the famous Las Vegas strip, yet technically in Paradise, Nevada. It was one of the newest stadiums in the NFL along with the Rams/Chargers SoFi stadium and Crystal Light. Our capacity was seventy thousand fans. Allegiant held sixty-five thousand and was also home to the UNLV Rebels college football team. In 2024, they hosted the Super Bowl, an accomplishment Crystal Light couldn't claim.

Currently, we're not in the running. For one thing, convincing the NFL that Lexington was a better location than larger markets wasn't easy. While the locations of future Super Bowls hadn't been announced beyond Atlanta in 2028, one of the rules for hosting a Super Bowl was to have enough hotel rooms within an hour's drive to accommodate thirty-five percent of the stadium's capacity. For us, that would mean nearly 25,000 rooms. Lexington had close to 12,000. Neighboring cities, such as Georgetown, Richmond, Frankfort, and Winchester added significantly to that number. Our facility was adequate. It was our supporting infrastructure that lacked.

It was a battle Dad vowed to keep fighting.

I stared up at the unique shape of Allegiant Stadium as it came into view. The structure was impressive. The domed roof allowed for natural light without the heat and rays of the desert sun. I'd been to this stadium before in a suite. Tomorrow will be my first time on the field under the dome.

DeQuinta stopped the car. He stepped out to open Grant's door while Virginia did the same for me.

The three of us walked without speaking across the large expanse of sidewalk to an entrance.

"Ms. Hubbard and Mr. Marsh from the Coopers," I said to a security guard.

"Yes," he replied after checking his tablet. "Let me show you inside." The guard explained the directions for us to reach our own respective locations. Once Grant went his own way, I let out a breath.

"Ms. Hubbard," the Raiders' vice president of operations said. "Welcome."

"Call me Vee, please."

"And I'm Chris. Now let me show you to…"

It was after six at night when Virginia and I returned to the hotel. Once we were up to my suite, I invited her inside. "I wasn't sure how this would go but thank you. It went well."

"I'm glad you're satisfied. We didn't have too much difficulty with reporters, seeing as the stadium was closed off to the public. Tomorrow will be different. I'll get you safely to and from the suite."

I shook my head. "I'm not staying in the suite with the rest of the family. I'll be on the sideline of the field."

Virginia opened her eyes wide. "I didn't know that."

"I'll be perfectly fine on the sideline. Allegiant has guards and security all around. The event is secure."

"When you leave the field?" she asked.

"I'll find a place where you can wait for me. If that's all right?"

"That will work. Do you plan to go out to dinner?"

"No," I said with relief as I kicked off my shoes. "I'm in for the night. I'll order room service and in the morning..." I looked at my watch. "I want to be to Allegiant by 9:00 a.m."

"The game isn't until one thirty."

"There's a lot that goes on before then."

Virginia smiled and nodded. "I'll be here at 8:45 a.m."

"Thank you."

After she was gone, I double-checked the door locks and looked around my suite.

CHAPTER 25

Vee

The Waldorf Astoria was situated in the heart of the Vegas strip but was a gambling-free hotel. Through the tall windows in my bedroom, I looked out upon the bright lights associated with the iconic city. My current view included Paris with the glowing Eiffel Tower replica, Planet Hollywood, and Aria.

As the host to many traveling NFL teams, this hotel was also secure. Judging by the time of evening, not a text from Fin, the players should be in the hotel. Currently, they would be in meetings with their offense, defense, or special team. In an hour or so, they would have a private dining room and a high-carb dinner. While these players were men, they had rules. Curfew was at 11:00 p.m.

Changing out of my work clothes, I donned soft pajama pants and a tank top when my phone rang. Leigh's name was on the screen.

"Hi," I answered.

"Hayden, Lip, and I are going to get dinner downstairs. Would you like to come along?"

I looked down at my change of clothes and smiled. "You are about ten minutes too late. I'm in comfy clothes and in for the night."

"Okay. We'll miss you."

"Thanks, Leigh."

"Vee, we're worried about you."

"Don't be. I'm not great with time change. I'll be good, I promise."

"All right. See you tomorrow?"

"On the plane home," I said, "if not before."

"Go Coopers."

"Go Coopers," I repeated.

Over three hours later, the remains of my dinner were on the dining table while I was curled up on the sofa with Bre's notes. She'd copied more of Dad's schedules. I was currently looking at the week before he died.

Among many other things listed, he had a call with an NFL International Office. He also had a meeting with Lexington city officials and a call with a representative from Under Armour. "What did you talk about?" I asked aloud.

I made a note to ask Bre for more information. There should be notes after each meeting. Knowing that Dad spoke to certain people wasn't helpful if I didn't know what was discussed.

I laid the papers on the coffee table. The small bottle of wine that came with my dinner was empty, replaced with a bottle of Evian. While it wasn't even ten o'clock, my eyes were tired and my temples throbbed.

My phone vibrated on the table beside me. A smile curled my lips at the sight of Fin's name. "You should be sleeping," I said as I answered the call. "You have a big game tomorrow."

"What's your room number?"

I sat forward. "Oh my God, Fin. You're not coming to my room."

"How much Fin's-in-control time have you had today?"

Shaking my head, I scoffed. "Not near enough. I'm headed to bed."

"I don't have much time until curfew, but I promise I can take some of that stress out of your voice. You just need to give me your room number."

"You can't hear my stress."

"I can," he said, his voice dropping an octave. "Don't make me ask again."

My nipples beaded at his deepening tone. "Promise me you won't be seen and photographed."

"I'll do my best."

With much reservation, I told him the number of my suite.

"You're closer than I thought. See you soon."

After disconnecting the call, I whispered, "This is a bad idea."

Bad idea or not, I hurried to the bathroom, brushed my teeth and splashed my already-washed face with water. I was brushing my hair when I heard the knock on the door. A quick peek out the peephole showed me a tall man with a Cincinnati baseball cap over his eyes.

Laughing for the first time all day, I opened the door and pulled him inside. "Did anyone see you?"

Fin palmed my cheeks and brought our lips together. His smile was panty melting and his blue orbs shone. "You're feeling better already, aren't you?"

"You're very cocky."

"Very, but if we start with that, I will definitely be late for curfew." He took off the baseball cap, lifted his head, and looked around the suite. "I need to renego-tiate my contract."

"That's not happening."

"Then tell me why I'm happy to have a room to myself and you have enough space up here for ten people."

"Ten people would be cramped."

Fin laughed. "You should try two grown football

players in a hotel room." He shook his head. "It's not pretty."

"Curfew is eleven?"

He looked down at his watch. "That gives me almost an hour."

"Share this stress relief you had planned."

"You're so fucking gorgeous." He teased the strap of my tank top and arched an eyebrow. "No bra, I approve."

My breathing deepened.

"I won't get to see you like this again until very late tomorrow night."

Taking a step back, I scanned from his leather shoes, his long legs covered with navy blue slacks, to his muscular torso and wide shoulders covered by a lighter blue button down. My gaze went higher yet to his square jaw covered with a day's worth of beard growth, to his sexy grin, and sparkling eyes. "Mr. Graham, you're quite handsome yourself."

"Come here," he said, taking my hand and leading me to the bedroom.

"I thought you said we didn't have time."

"This is Fin's-in-control time."

"I don't want you to get in trouble, and I sure don't want anyone to know where you—"

Once we crossed the threshold, his lips covered mine, stopping my concerns from coming forth. This wasn't like our hello kiss. Now, in the bedroom, with his arm wrapped around my waist and my hips tugged against his, our bodies melded together, soft against hard. Our tongues danced as my senses filled with sandalwood and my circulation raced. By the time we pulled apart for air, I was breathless. "I don't remember what I was saying."

Fin smiled, his cheeks rising and small lines forming near his eyes. "You were saying, yes, Fin. Whatever you say."

It was my turn to grin. "I'm pretty sure that wasn't what I was saying."

"Lie down on the bed on your stomach."

I tilted my head in question.

"Ms. Hubbard, we don't have time for you to question my methods."

Scooting onto the covers, I crawled to the middle of the mattress and lay with my head near the foot of the bed. "This feels a little scandalous."

He moved a pillow from the head to the foot. "Here."

I pulled it under my head and shoulders. "Oh," I said loudly as Fin's long fingers stroked my neck.

"I'm warming the muscles," he said.

My body reacted as his strokes morphed to kneading and circular motions.

A massage.

That was his secret weapon.

Closing my eyes, the tension I hadn't admitted was present began to ease from my tightened body. Squeezing and rolling my muscles, Fin's strong hands worked out knots of stress. My hums and noises of approval filled the air.

Fin's attention went lower to my back and waist. He had me lulled into a state of semi-consciousness, when he tugged the waistband of my soft pants down. Cool air startled me.

"Fin?"

"Trust me."

I wiggled, allowing him to fully remove the pajama pants and my panties, fully aware he had a bird's eye view of my behind.

"Up on your knees."

How much time has passed?

If I argued, I wouldn't find out his plan. I had to admit that so far, his plan was working. With my curiosity piqued and my tension waning, I hugged the pillow and complied. A moan escaped my lips as those strong fingers that were massaging my flesh were skillfully eased between my folds.

"You're wet."

"Fin."

"Trust me. A good orgasm is the best stress reliever." He playfully swatted my raised ass. "Roll over, Vee. I'm going to give you the orgasm you need."

"I-I..."

His hand again connected with my ass. This time with more of a sting.

"Ouch."

"Roll over."

The back of my head landed on the soft pillow as Fin spread my knees and buried his face in my pussy. There was no warming up—no easing into this. My hips bucked, and I screamed out as he nipped my clit and lapped my essence. Fire came to life within me, a smoldering ember that with the mere striking of his tongue and fingers ignited a raging blaze. Flares detonated throughout my nervous system as the kindling of my flesh singed from his searing touch.

"Fuck me, Fin," I cried out, desperately pleading. I didn't know how much time we had. I only knew one thing. I needed him inside me. I wanted his closeness, to feel his heart beating in his chest and to share the same breaths.

The mattress shifted as the sound of Fin's zipper filled my body with anticipation. "Back on your knees, Vee."

Scurrying to comply, I rolled, again hugging the soft pillow. While we weren't face-to-face, the scandalous nature of our rendezvous came back to me as Fin pierced me, thrusting deep inside my wet core, stretching me to a delicious sense of fullness.

"Vee, this is going to be fast." His warm breath was on my neck. "Don't hold it against me."

"You said Garcia wanted you to be faster in the pocket. Consider this practice."

His baritone laugh filled the air.

Fin's hands roamed beneath my tank top until he seized my hips, pumping faster and faster. Our labored breaths combined with moans and whimpers echoed throughout the suite. It was as his hand lowered to my clit that my entire body exploded, a series of detonations, from my scalp to my toes. I fell to the bed, my knees giving out with Fin over the top of me.

His lips came to my cheek with butterfly kisses. "I didn't come here for sex. I truly came here to relieve the stress I could hear in your voice."

I craned my neck. "You did it." My eyes opened wide. "What time is it?"

Fin shifted, breaking our union. "It's 10:54." His smile radiated in his loving gaze. "If I get reprimanded, I'll have to confess."

"You will do no such thing. I promised Tilson our relationship wouldn't affect our working together."

Fin stood, pulling up his boxer shorts and pants.

Staring in disbelief, I shook my head. "You're still wearing your shoes. And, well, everything."

He reached down and cupped my cheeks. "There's the smile I adore. Power play is hard to pass up." He kissed my nose. "Get a good night's sleep."

Rolling over, I stretched across the bed. "You too."

By the time I had my pajama pants back in place, Fin was gone. Locking the door, I leaned against it with a smile I wouldn't have predicted an hour earlier. With my gaze toward the ceiling, I said, "Don't let him get caught."

It was then I noticed my water bottle was missing. After turning out the lights, I crawled into the large bed and sent Fin a text.

"DID YOU STEAL MY WATER BOTTLE?"

HIS ANSWER CAME RIGHT AWAY.

"IT WAS A PROP. I WAS OUT OF THE ROOM FOR WATER. Smiling emoji. IT WORKED. NO CONFESSION NECESSARY."

I SHOOK MY HEAD.

"IT FEELS LIKE WE'RE KIDS SNEAKING AROUND."

. . .

"KEEP SMILING. I'LL BE WATCHIING YOU TOMORROW ON THE SIDELINES."

"WATCH THE BIG GUYS WHO WANT TO KNOCK YOU DOWN."

CLOSING MY EYES, I fell sound asleep.

CHAPTER 26

Fin

The on-field warm-up was over. The rush of adrenaline was flowing, a familiar feeling that I wasn't certain I was ready to stop experiencing. Back in the locker room, Coach Tilson's pregame peptalk was more of what we'd been hearing since Wednesday. The Raiders' defense was better than good. Our offense had to be even better; it could be, it would be. Our offensive line—the tackles, guards, and center needed to be impenetrable. Our eligible receivers were to run their assigned routes and guard against the interception. My assignment was to read the defense, call the plays accordingly, and avoid turnovers.

Their offense was equally good. Their 4–1 record showed it. That meant our defense had to push them out of their comfort zone. Read the plays. The Raiders were known for their ground game. While the tackles and ends needed to rush, the secondary couldn't let down their guard for a long pass. Our linebackers were the quarterbacks of the defensive line. Their primary role was to stop everything—block the run, cover receivers, and blitz the quarterback.

"We've got this, Coach," came as a testosterone-fueled pledge.

"You're the Coopers," Tilson screamed. "You've got this. You're going to show those fans out there that Lexington should never be underestimated."

"We've got this, Coach."

The locker room doors opened, and we followed Coach Tilson through the tunnel and out to the field. Each player had their own pregame ritual. Some players prayed while others meditated. Others hyped the adrenaline with jumps and grunts, often with their special playlist blaring in their ears. There was no right way to prepare yourself mentally for the start of a game.

As the national anthem resonated through Allegiant Stadium, I closed my eyes for my ritual. Ever since I played Division II, my thoughts at the beginning of a game went back to my father. Dad was my and Zane's coach when we were young. He wasn't coaching elite athletes. Dad was coaching children. While he wanted them to learn, what he sought more was sharing the love of football, of the game. His pregame mantra was a directive to accomplish three objectives throughout the game.

Learn something—anything.

Never give up.

Play your absolute best, better than your last game, but not as good as your next.

Dad didn't emphasize winning or losing. Winning, he said, would come when you accomplished the three given objectives.

As the singer hit the high notes, I vowed to learn something today—I'd been working on the tells Pickett clued me into. Today, I would put them to practice. I also wouldn't give up and would do my absolute best.

"Graham," Tilson yelled, "you and Johnson are out on the field for the coin flip. Now."

Malik and I jogged across the field to the official at the fifty-yard line. We were met by two Raiders' players, their quarterback, Joe Williams, and their safety, Jalan Kelly. We shook hands and introduced ourselves to one another.

"Good afternoon, captains," the official said. "Here is our coin." He rotated it in his fingers. "This is heads. This is tails. Coopers, you are the visitors. You will call the toss. What is your call, heads or tails?"

Malik and I looked at one another. We'd already decided. I was the one to speak. "The Coopers choose heads."

"Your call is heads."

"Yes," we said in unison.

The official took a step back, tossed the coin into the air. It landed on the ground. "It is tails. Raiders win the coin flip." He looked at the Raiders' captains. "Do you want to receive or defer."

"Defer," Williams said.

"The Raiders will defer," the official announced. "The Coopers will receive first. Let's have a good game."

We jogged back to the team, and I took a moment to admire the woman on the sideline, the one wearing the amber dress with cowboy boots. The same one who last night was wearing a thin shirt and nothing more. Vee nodded in my direction. It was barely perceivable, but I saw it as our kicking return team took the field.

I noticed Vee checking her watch as the Raiders' kicker sent the ball long and high. The Raiders' special team had time to make it down the field, circling the ball as it landed near the five-yard line. It didn't stop, bouncing into the end zone—a touchback. I exhaled. Disastrous field position avoided.

Pratt was in my face as I pulled down my helmet. "You've got this, Graham. Read the defense and play our game. You've got the arm for the long pass, and you're surrounded with the best in the game for handoffs." He patted my shoulder pads. "Show them what you've got—what the Coopers got."

The offense met in a huddle. The play coming inside my helmet from Coach Pratt was an RPO—run play option. That meant my receivers and tight ends would run their routes. If they weren't open, we'd opt for the running play. I made the call. At the end I yelled, "For Reid."

"For Reid," my teammates yelled.

We lined up in shotgun formation on our own thirty-yard line. The Raiders' defense scrambled. I set the cadence. "Set, hut!"

The ball was snapped and in my hands. I stepped back, reading my progressions. Kylon Lewis, the wide receiver on the right, ran a flag route. The Raiders' defense wasn't expecting a long pass as the first play. Lewis was open. My arm reared back and I threw the ball.

The O-line had given me time. The tackle came seconds after the ball left my hand. The deafening Raiders' crowd went silent as Lewis caught the pass, going out of bounds at the Raiders' forty-two-yard line. A pickup of twenty-eight yards.

"Move, move," came through my helmet.

I motioned to our players to get into formation. We had the unbeatable Raiders scratching their asses and a no-huddle offense would hopefully keep them that way. I handed the ball to Dijon. The O-line held open a gap long enough for him to run six yards.

"Keep going," Pratt said in my ear. "We're in field-goal range. It's the first play of the game. Let's get some numbers on the board."

Another no-huddle offense. "Set, hut!"

A shovel pass to Morgan, our fullback. He caught it and went out of bounds at the thirty-two-yard line. Another first down.

Whistles blew and yellow flags hit the ground.

"Fuck, holding," came through my helmet.

The crowd cheered at the call, resulting in a Coopers' ten-yard penalty. Now instead of a first down at the thirty-two, we had a third and fourteen at the forty-seven-yard line.

I agreed with the voice in my helmet. This was too far for a field goal. Pratt wanted another pass. This time we huddled, and I called the pass play, a play option. "Gun, right, tight, trey right, jet sweep, option, for Reid."

"For Reid."

Our 11-personnel offense was designed to create matchup problems for the defense. I set the cadence. "Set. Hut!"

Lewis ran go route. Patel ran corner route. JD ran dig route, and Treshawn ran out route. I read the progressions. The secondary defense was covering the players farther down the field. I threw the ball to JD. As he caught it near the forty-yard line, I was laid out by one of their tackles—or maybe it was a Greyhound bus.

I stared up at the dome for a moment, trying to catch my breath. For a moment, it felt like an elephant was sitting on my chest. There were even stars twinkling up above.

"Fin, you all right?" Jamir asked as he helped me to my feet.

I grimaced as the shrill sound of whistles filled the air. "Fuck, yeah, I'm good."

"The call's on them," Jamir said.

"Graham," came from my helmet. "You're out."

Out?

What the fuck?

I attempted deep breaths as I made my way to the sideline. As Simpson went out, I heard the announcement.

"Roughing the passer," came from the speakers. "Defense, number 77, fifteen-yard penalty. Automatic first down."

"I'm fine," I screamed at Pratt. I turned to Tilson. "Why am I out?"

Garcia grabbed my arm. "You took a hard hit. You're going in the blue tent."

"Fuck, I'm fine."

He wasn't listening.

CHAPTER 27

Vee

My play call list nearly shredded with my intense grip as Coopers' training staff helped Fin into the blue tent. In my ear, Drew was calling the play to Simpson. On the field, our players were lined up in split formation at the thirty-two-yard line. Simpson had the ball. He handed it off to Morgan, who dodged defensive players and made it to the twenty-six-yard line.

While my attention was on the field, I couldn't help watching the blue tent. The flap was still closed. "Please be okay," I said softly.

Back on the field, Simpson had the ball. He was dancing behind the line of scrimmage. The ball was in the air. Patel caught the ball while dragging his toes before being pushed out of bounds. Whistles blew.

The tension in my neck reminded me of Fin's stress-relief methods from last night.

"Unnecessary roughness. Defense. Number 94. Fifteen-yard penalty. The ball will be placed at the sixteen-yard line. First down."

The crowd inside Allegiant Stadium booed loudly, unhappy with the call. I watched the jumbotron for the replay. Patel's feet were both down and in bounds when number 94 plowed him to the ground out of bounds.

Clenching my jaw, I tried not to show my disgust. The Raiders were playing dirty. For once, I was happy to hear the whistles.

It took six more plays to score.

Touchdown Coopers.

When I turned, I saw Fin sitting on the bench and let out a relieved breath. If he was not in the locker room, that meant he didn't require further medical attention. Hopefully, he'd be put back in the game after the Raiders' possession. I looked up at the clock. Our time of possession was over eight minutes. And we came out of it with seven points.

I clapped as our defense took the field.

Our defense nearly intercepted a long pass. I held my breath waiting for a pass interference call. While the receiver clearly wanted one, the officials didn't comply. The Raiders were third and six. My nails carved half-moons into my palms as I clenched my fists.

The ball was snapped.

Johnson, one of our cornerbacks, ran around the line of scrimmage for a sack.

Raiders' time of possession was only two minutes. They had no choice but to punt.

My smile couldn't be restrained when I saw Fin putting on his helmet. He was back in the game. By halftime we were up 10–3. I wasn't ready to celebrate quite yet.

The Raiders came out of halftime with a boulder on their shoulders. They had first possession, which resulted in another field goal. The score was now 10–6. Fin continued as quarterback. Hearing the play call in my headset, I realized I was watching not just Fin, but anticipating who he would give the ball to, and if it would be a handoff or a pass play.

In the fourth quarter, we had the ball in the red zone, with a first and goal from the four-yard line. The Raiders' defense was solid. They stopped us on the first, second, and third downs. Drew called for the kicking team to go out onto the field.

Fin shouted at the offense. I couldn't hear, but from what I could see, he was telling them to stay. I could only hear Drew's voice. I squinted my eyes at the tirade he was screaming at Fin.

Fin huddled the offense.

Drew withdrew the kicking team.

Our offense lined up. The Raiders' defense was tight.

Fin handed the ball to Bennett. The defense swarmed.

The official's arms went up, indicating a touchdown, but I didn't understand how. Bennett had been stopped.

"Oh my God." It was a quarterback scramble.

Fin hadn't handed the ball off.

Bennett's fake deserved an Oscar nomination. I looked up at the jumbotron to see Fin tucking the ball and running wide around the line of scrimmage. The Coopers' players on the sideline and field were celebrating.

The extra point attempt was blocked. The Coopers were up 16–6 with less than five minutes remaining. The Raiders had possession of the ball. Their quarterback's passes were on point. In less than two minutes, with multiple first downs they were to our four-yard line.

Coach Brown sent in Wood, our 6 feet, 1 inch and 210-pound nickelback. In my ear, Brown was screaming at Lester, the Coopers' linebacker. I checked my play sheet, not as familiar with defense as offense. Our defensive coordinator was calling for a 5-man rush.

The ball was snapped.

Our defense lunged forward. Wood found the gap

and tackled Williams. The Raiders' quarterback was sacked again. They were now second and goal on the eleven-yard line. The Raiders' offense lined up again with no-huddle offense. Williams handed off the ball. Their fullback ran nearly to the goal line. It was more progress than Brown wanted.

The call was third and inches.

There was time for one more play before the two-minute warning.

The Raiders' scored.

At the two-minute warning, we were still ahead, but only by three points. A touchdown would beat us. A field goal would tie.

Fin and the offense were back on the field. I didn't take a full breath until the final buzzer. While each team had a possession during the final two minutes, neither team scored. The final score was 16–13; Coopers won. Not only was it a win, but the Coopers scored sixteen points against a team that on average only gave up 4.4 points a game.

"Great game," I said to the players as they headed into the locker room.

"Thanks, Ms. Maeve."

When I turned toward the field, I watched Fin with his helmet in hand, speaking with a reporter. A smile tugged at my lips. His hair was a mess, and he had a few scratches and bruises from the battle, but in my opinion, he was still the most handsome man on the field and beyond.

"Ms. Hubbard."

I turned to find a camera in my face. I lifted my hand and tucked my face down. "Speak to the players. They won the game."

"Just one question."

I shook my head as someone tugged on my arm. It was Virginia.

"Ms. Hubbard, we need to go now."

My pulse was rapid as she walked me off the field down the tunnel toward the locker rooms. We didn't stop until she walked me past the locker room and other reporters. They shouted questions, but my ears were buzzing too loudly to hear their words.

When we came to a stop, I tried to hide the fact that I was trembling. "Thank you. I wasn't expecting that."

"It's my job," she said with a smile. "Let's get you up to the suite. Someone from the Raiders' organization showed me a back elevator."

The giant void Dad left came back with gut-wrenching speed. I hadn't thought about him during the game. Now it was as if I'd just learned of his death. I shook my head. I didn't want to face the family, not yet. "I'd like to go to the plane."

"I'll call for a car."

Once we were in the car, I sent a text message to Leigh.

. . .

"I'M HEADED TO THE PLANE. WE'LL LEAVE AS SOON AS EVERYONE GETS THERE. THANKS FOR PASSING ON THIS MESSAGE."

LEIGH REPLIED WITH A THUMBS-UP EMOJI.

My temples throbbed and my skin felt tight as I worked to contain the sudden onset of emotion. After thanking Virginia again for her help, I climbed the steps to the Gulfstream and was met by Susan and our pilot, Tony.

"Welcome, Ms. Hubbard. Congratulations on the win. Will the others be arriving soon?"

The win. I was losing my mind. I'd forgotten about the win. "Others? Oh, coming. I hope so." Carrying my leather bag, I made my way back to the four-person table.

Susan came closer. "I was about to convert the table into a bed for Mrs. Hubbard. We won't arrive in Lexington until about one in the morning. She likes to sleep."

"You know what? The recliners recline. There's no sense in having one passenger monopolize seating for four. We have eight passengers on this trip."

Her eyes opened wider. "Are you sure?"

I pulled my laptop from my bag and placed it on the table. "I'm certain. I'd also like a cosmo, please."

"Right away."

Since Fin's relaxation methods couldn't help me through this flight, I chose alcohol. It wouldn't clear my head, but it just might keep me sane. Anyway, it was more than likely the rest of the family had been imbibing throughout the game. I'd only swallowed my first sip of the tart, fruity cocktail when through the window I watched two cars approaching the plane on the tarmac. "Susan, may I have a second before takeoff?"

"Sure thing, Ms. Hubbard."

The stem of the second cocktail glass was in my fingers as the clangor of voices filled the cabin. Daphne stopped in her tracks. "Susan, where's the bed?"

I lifted my glass in a toasting motion. "Good game. Daphne, we have eight people on this flight. I decided a four-person space didn't need to be reserved for only one person. Enjoy a recliner."

"Ah. I..." She stammered as she looked around, truly puzzled.

Leigh, Hayden, and Lip were all smiles as they joined me at the table. "What did you think of the game?" I asked, my bout of mourning safely subdued.

"It was great," Lip replied. "We not only won, but we also beat the spread."

Hayden said, "The most any team has scored on

the Raiders this season was seven points. The Coopers scored sixteen."

Leigh tilted her head. "Will that be Fin's last game?"

The reminder filled me with mixed emotions. He was safer on the bench. However, I knew how much this season has meant to him, especially after last year's in LA. "It will be his last game to start, assuming Dennison stays healthy."

Grant appeared next to the table. "With Dennison healthy, we should consider letting either Graham or Simpson go."

The vodka in my cosmo was racing through my circulation, fueling my response. "It's not on the table."

He shook his head dismissively.

I lowered my half-filled glass to the table and looked pointedly at Grant. "If Dennison would God-forbid be injured again, then I suppose you would want us to rehire the QB we let go, at an even higher price?"

He shrugged. "It's something to think about. Dennison won't get hurt again." He walked away as Susan announced that Tony was ready to take off.

"You can be kind of fierce," Lip whispered.

"What I am is pissed. Let's make it through Tuesday's service and after that, all bets are off." I swallowed the remainder of my cosmo and handed my empty glass to Susan. "I'm going to need dinner before another one of those."

She nodded. "As soon as we're at cruising altitude."

"Thank you."

A few minutes later, she brought a basket of dinner rolls and sat them in the middle of the table with a wink.

"You're the best, Susan." Turning to those around the table, I said, "There's no buffet on the sideline."

CHAPTER 28

Fin

My Monday morning alarm came too early, especially considering the team's plane didn't return to Lexington until nearly two in the morning. Though I didn't want to wake Vee last night, I went to her place not mine. There was a pull to spend time with her I couldn't resist.

When I arrived, Vee was sound asleep. Even the beeping of the security alarm didn't rouse her. Images of our secret rendezvous Saturday night were playing in my mind, mixed in between memories of her on the sideline. Despite my desire to touch her, I couldn't make myself wake her.

"Make it stop," she said sleepily at the chime of the alarm.

Reaching for my phone reminded me that I'd been run over by a bus yesterday. After I turned it off, Vee curled her body into mine. Kissing the top of her hair, I wrapped my arm around her. Ignoring the tenderness in my side and chest, I said, "This seems like a recipe for being late to Maker's Mark."

Her warm hands came to my bare chest as she blinked her gorgeous eyes. "I didn't know if you'd come here or go to your place." Her lips curled. "I approve of your decision."

"You were out last night. I don't think you even heard the security system beep."

Vee rolled away. Staring up at the ceiling, she sighed. "Leigh and Hayden brought me home last night." She lifted her fingers to her temples. "I think Hayden drove my rental and Leigh brought me home."

I widened my eyes. "You think?"

"It's all a bit fuzzy."

My laugh filled the bedroom as I sat up, leaning over her. "Ms. Hubbard, were you drunk?"

Her gaze met mine as she grimaced. "I mean, legally—possibly. Let's just say that it was a good choice not to drive."

I brushed my lips over hers, inhaling a sour vodka aroma. "Cosmos?"

Vee nodded.

"How many?"

Pressing her lips together, she shrugged. Then her eyes opened wide. "Shit, what time is it?"

"My alarm was set for six."

Shoving me away, Vee threw back the bed covers. "I'm supposed to meet with Don at seven this morning." She hurried toward the bathroom. "I'll shower fast, and I should make it."

My torso made its presence known as I sat up on the edge of the mattress. I was reminded of what I told Vee after her car accident. The next day is always worse. Shrugging it off, I followed the trail of Vee's sleep clothes into the bathroom. My cheeks rose in a grin at finding her naked at the vanity brushing her teeth. The shower was running, no doubt warming the water. Lifting my arm to the door jamb, I stared at her round ass.

Her stunning green stare met my gaze in the mirror and she shook her head.

"I just wondered why you're meeting Coach Tilson so early."

Vee spit and rinsed before turning toward me, completely nude, disheveled, and sexy enough to harden my already-hard morning wood.

Her smile dimmed as she looked down at my chest. "You're bruised."

I rubbed my fingers over my breastbone. "I keep telling you big guys want to knock me down."

"But you're okay?"

"I'm fine. They checked me out in the tent. Why are you meeting with Coach Tilson so early?"

"He told me last week that he and Dad had standing Monday morning meetings where they discussed the game without anyone else. He said he'd be to my office today at seven." She walked toward the shower and opened the glass door. "I need to hurry." Her eyebrows arched as her eyes pointedly looked down to my erection, not well hidden under my nylon shorts. "If not, I'd help you with that problem you have."

I walked toward her with a grin. "I'm sure you could explain to Coach that you are going to be late."

Vee shook her head. "Past experience tells me that you'll be erect again. This is my first day-after-game meeting as owner, and I don't want to be late."

Leaning down, I brought my lips to hers. The vodka scent was replaced by minty freshness. "Let me get you some coffee."

"Only coffee," she said, stepping into the steamy stall. "I'll worry about food after my meeting."

I let out a long breath and watched as she stepped under the warm spray. I feared the familiarity Vee and I shared in the past would never be resurrected, yet it had, as effortlessly as slipping on a glove. We missed fourteen years of each other's lives. Watching her lather her long hair, I wondered if maybe as devastating as it had been all those years ago, perhaps the end result was better. We both had our lives on our own terms. We were no longer children with ideals. We were adults who knew life's ups and downs. It was time to find out what life could be together.

Her silhouette through the glass and steam was perfect. The Greek goddess Aphrodite, renowned for her grace, allure, and supreme physical perfection, had nothing on Vee. "I could join you," I offered with a grin.

"No." Her answer was immediate.

Chuckling to myself, I wondered if my day would get better or worse after starting out with a full-out rejection. On my way to the kitchen, I decided the view I'd just enjoyed was a sufficient consolation prize.

Vee was dressed and blow drying her hair by the time the coffee brewed. Stepping into the bathroom, I was bombarded with the sweet aromas of lotion, shampoo, and perfume.

"I found a travel cup," I said, setting the hot Coopers' cup on the vanity. "I figured you could take it to go. Cream no sugar."

She turned off the dryer and turned to me. "Thank you. I didn't get a chance to tell you good game."

"Yeah, you did."

Vee tilted her face in question. "We haven't spoken since Saturday night."

I reached for her waist and brought our hips together. "Every time I looked at you during the game. You were all sexy in that dress and cowboy boots." My smile grew. "Every time I made eye contact with you, you were telling me what you thought."

"I think I was more nervous about winning than I've been all season." She took a ragged breath.

"Why was that?"

She shrugged. "It was the first game without Dad. I was afraid if the Coopers lost, it would be held against me."

"By whom?"

Vee shook her head. "We can talk tonight." Her eyes opened wide. "Unless you're ready for some alone time. I'd under—"

My finger landed gently on her lips. "I want to be with you."

Her smile returned. "Good. That's what I want."

"It's 6:35 a.m."

"I'm hurrying," she said, turning the blow dryer back on.

I was sitting at the kitchen island with my tablet as Vee came out of the bedroom looking beautiful and professional. Her hair hung in a long braid over her shoulder. The little bit of makeup she'd added and the emerald-green blouse caused her eyes to pop. The bruise on her cheek was almost invisible. Black slacks and high heels and a soft white button sweater completed her look.

A light cloud of sweetness engulfed me as she came close and kissed my cheek.

"I'll see you tonight."

"I could drive you if you're still tipsy."

She swatted my shoulder. "I'm not. Don't tell secrets."

I lifted my right hand. "I solemnly swear."

Vee's cheeks rose and her green orbs shone. "I trust you." She turned around and grabbed her leather bag off the sofa and disappeared out the front door.

I wasn't needed at the football center this early, but that didn't mean I shouldn't get ready. It was closer to eight thirty when I pulled up in the line to enter the parking lot. Shaking my head, I saw the news trucks and reporters standing on the side of the road. "Give up," I said under my breath.

"Graham," Coach Tilson said as I entered the locker room.

"Yeah?"

"Lacy Reynolds is expecting you in the trainer's office."

She was a certified athletic trainer and a physician's assistant who had completed my physical when I first came to the Coopers.

"I'm fine. I was checked out on the field."

The coach lifted his eyebrow. "Go see her before film at nine."

Exhaling, I acquiesced. "Okay."

After hanging my jacket and tossing my duffel bag into my locker, I saw Troy Dennison coming toward me. "You ready to retake the spotlight?" I asked.

He flashed me with a million-dollar smile. "You know it. How about you?"

"Front seat to legend making." I meant what I said. The warrior in me wanted to start. The man nearing thirty-seven years old was ready to take the back seat. "Tilson is sending me over to Lacy. Apparently, they're worried about me."

"That's a good thing. The Coopers give a shit about all the players. I was upset when I was placed on the IR, missing four weeks." He nodded. "But now I'm back and I feel good."

"Glad to hear it. I'll see you in films."

The large room in the training center was buzzing with various players who were feeling the aftereffects of our tough game.

"How are you feeling, Fin?" Lacy asked as I entered.

I flashed her my best smile. "I feel too good to be examined."

She pressed her lips together. "Well, I'm not asking. You took a big hit yesterday. We need to run a few tests. What about soreness?"

"You're not asking," I said with a smirk. "Are we talking about nonconsensual examinations?"

"You consented when you signed your contract. Soreness?"

"A little. My chest and side are bruised." I lifted my right arm, showing Lacy the underside of my forearm. "Some abrasions."

"Come back to an exam room and let me see your chest."

"I can strip right here." I looked around. "Most people in this room have seen me naked."

"I don't need you naked, Fin. Come with me."

I did as she said. Once she closed the door, I removed my shirt. "I'm fine."

She came closer and lifted her fingers to my chest. Her eyes narrowed as she took in the contusion. "Any trouble breathing?"

"No."

"How about pain?" She pushed on my sides.

I winced in one spot. "Okay, that spot is tender."

Lacy reached for my wrist. "Your pulse is rapid." Looking at her watch, she continued to hold my wrist. "It's ninety beats per minute."

"That's within the normal range."

"Not for an athlete like you. It could be a symptom of something else." She pressed her lips together. "I'd like to do an x-ray and CT scan."

"Why?"

"You could have a broken rib. The CT scan will look at your lungs and heart."

"Lacy, I'm fine."

"That's what we'll find out."

CHAPTER 29

Vee

A few hours earlier

T he sky was still dark as I made my way to Maker's Mark. The bright side was it must have also been too early for the reporters. I made it onto the grounds with nothing more than a wave. I'd just sat down at my desk when there was a knock on my office door. Being also too early for Jen or anyone else to be in the outer office, I anticipated my visitor and called out, "Come in."

Don Tilson arrived with two paper cups of coffee in hand. "You're here." He'd never been one for pleasantries.

"I am." I stood and took a cup. "Don, let's sit over here." I motioned to the comfortable chairs and sofa near the windows. "Tell me. How long do these meetings typically last?" I sat in a singular chair and crossed my ankles beneath my chair.

Don Tilson sat in another singular chair, sitting forward with his legs spread. We were separated by a small table holding a green silk plant that looked remarkably real. Beyond the windowpanes a rosy hue began to crack in the eastern horizon, signs that the day was beginning.

Don replied, "That depends on how upset or happy Reid was."

Nodding my head, I removed the coffee lid. Seeing the black coffee, I blew on the contents. "I was wondering, was it all about Dad's thoughts or did you provide your own?"

"It went both ways."

I straightened my neck and shoulders and took the bull by the horns. "What did you think of yesterday's play?"

"We won."

Putting the coffee on the small table to cool, I nodded. "We did. Any concerns?"

Tilson sat back, crossing his ankle over his other knee. "The Coopers need to keep improving. Dennison is back to full pads. Although with the bye and tomorrow's service, he won't get back into the action until Saturday."

"No doubt you'll get him in game-day shape."

"How do you feel about Graham going back to second place?"

"Don, are you asking me that as the owner of the Coopers or as someone who knows Griffin Graham well?"

He wrinkled his brow. "Both, if I'm being honest."

"If you were honest with my father, I expect no less now."

"You're okay with the demotion?"

I shrugged. "I don't see it as a demotion. If Mr. Graham does, then he wasn't paying attention. And to the contrary, I believe he has been paying attention. He was signed as a possible third string. His performance, and nothing else, resulted in his contract renegotiation. Troy Dennison's injury thrust Graham into the first-place position. It's my opinion that while he did exceptionally well in that role, Troy Dennison is our star player. First-round pick. I can't imagine a man with as much time in the league as Graham would have any difficulty understanding the way a roster works. First and foremost, Dennison is the Coopers' quarterback."

Tilson took a drink of his coffee.

"I've reviewed tape from yesterday," he said. "The two Raiders' penalty calls against Graham and Patel weren't the only dirty plays. The majority went uncalled."

"Do you have the video evidence?"

He nodded. "We have a list of names headed to the

training center to be checked out. The Raiders' defense was brutal."

I remembered the dark purple bruise on Fin's chest. "Who are you sending to be checked out?"

"I can send you a list."

"Graham?" I was almost afraid to ask. "He was checked out in the tent."

Tilson lowered his foot to the floor and sat forward. "It isn't always protocol to double-check injuries. Is there a reason you're concerned?"

"I'm concerned with all our players. Graham and Patel took violent hits. I believe they should be reexamined. So should anyone involved with the plays you have marked on video. Show your concerns to Beasley, Darin Marsh, Drew, and Darius. If they agree, we'll draft a formal review request with the league."

"You don't want to see the film?"

I inhaled. "Something my father emphasized was the importance of a skilled staff, people he not only trusted but knew could carry the mantle when needed. Your position on the executive staff is needed, Don. Dad trusted you. I will too unless you give me a reason not to. Consult with others in football operations. Send me the names, plays, and film clips of what you and the others unanimously believe deserve review."

Don started to speak, but I jumped in. "Speaking of defense. Malik Johnson and Tyler Wood were on fire, each with a sack. I'm sure you know Williams averages four sacks a season. Yesterday, he was sacked twice in one day."

"Unfortunately, Xavien Martin, our—"

"Defensive end," I interjected.

"Yeah." He looked surprised. "Well, he's being evaluated for a knee injury."

"Do you think he'll be out long?"

"It depends. That's up to the docs."

I remembered the practice Fin came home sore from. "I watched an offense practice against our practice defense squad last week. There's a player, Marcel Pickett." I nodded. "He's fast and I've heard smart. Darius should look at him. We'll move him up if necessary."

"Our starting roster is full."

I nodded. "We'll see after the IR comes out. Pickett was impressive."

Don's eyebrows arched. "I'll make a note about him. Last week you were concerned with conservative play calling," Don said. "What are your thoughts on this week?"

"Not as concerned. Our offense kept the run and pass plays going. The quarterback sneak in the fourth quarter was shocking. Visually, I followed Bennett into the pile. I didn't even notice that Graham ran the ball into the end zone until the touchdown was called."

"You mentioned Tyler Wood," Don said. "What were your thoughts on that play?"

I felt as if I were taking a test. If that was the case, I was damn well going to pass. "You're talking about during the fourth quarter, putting Wood in as nickelback. Brilliant. That extra push gave the defense the power for a 5-man rush. Better yet, the play worked. It showed our strength on defense. I think it was a good play call."

Tilson shared one of his rare smiles. "You watch the game—really watch."

"I'm going to continue to do so from the sideline. When I'm there, the game is all-encompassing. There are too many distractions in the suite. After home games, I try to rewatch it on television. I want to hear what the announcers are saying."

He chuckled. "Mostly talking shit."

"I appreciate other perspectives."

"Vee, I'm being honest. I'd be lying if I said I wasn't worried about the Coopers' future if you take over."

The small hairs on the back of my neck stood to attention. "I am the owner, Don. There's no *if*."

Don pressed his lips together and nodded. "I wasn't finished." He bobbed his head. "May I?"

"Please, go on."

"Young lady..."

I saw red while at the same time I was doing my best to keep my resting-bitch face at bay.

He continued, "I believe you could prove me and others wrong. Your daddy thought you could hang the moon and the stars." His rare smile returned. "For now, I'm going to trust Reid's decision, and I'll talk to others about doing the same."

Relief came in a wave, releasing my growing resentment of the unbridled misogyny that abounded within this organization. While I passed this test, I had no illusion that Don Tilson, Royce Beasley, or even Uncle Darin would ever fully believe in me.

I'd take this as one battle won.

The war had yet to fully begin.

Smiling a closed-lip smile, I stood. "Don, thank you for this meeting." I offered him my hand and we shook. "Please get those tapes and names to me before noon. I'd like to move fast on approaching the league for official reviews. Also, I need the names on our current injury report before they go to the press. And I'll see you next Monday morning?"

"We have a bye."

"I'm sure we can find things to chat about. I'll bring the coffee."

"I'll be here, Ms. Hubbard."

"Vee is acceptable. Have a nice day."

I waited until Don was gone and the door shut before letting out a long breath. The meeting had been a small victory, hopefully enough to sustain me through this morning's executive meeting.

Taking Don's black coffee into my attached bathroom, I wrinkled my nose, poured it down the sink, and went to the front office.

"Good morning?" Jen said. "I was surprised to see Coach Tilson leave. I didn't know you were in yet." She looked at her watch. "It's early."

"It is. For the next twelve weeks I have a standing meeting with Coach Tilson every Monday morning at seven." I looked around, smelling a delicious brew. "You haven't by chance started making coffee, have you?"

Jen smiled. "Coming right up."

"I'll be happy to get it myself." I walked toward the decadent aroma and poured a cup, complete with cream from the refrigerator. I stopped at Jen's desk with my fingers wrapped around the warm mug. "Would you please make a call to Rachel Marsh's assistant and ask if Rachel can come speak to me once she's in. I'd like to talk before the meeting."

"Right away."

Carrying my coffee back to my office, I set it on the desk. Next to my landline phone was a manilla folder I didn't remember seeing before and hadn't noticed earlier. Opening it, I found lists of names, phone numbers, and email addresses. These included the NFL commissioner and other NFL owners. My forehead wrinkled as I carried it out to Jen.

"Where did this folder come from?"

"Bre Stanton brought it to you late Friday. You were gone."

"Did she tell you anything about it?"

Jen shook her head. "She said it was for you and asked if she could put it on your desk."

"She didn't give it to you?" A strange sense of violation sent goose bumps scattering over my flesh.

Jen's expression turned puzzled. "Vee, I told her it was okay to set that on your desk. She's brought other things down from your father's office. I'm sorry. Is that now a problem?"

My mind was filled with pictures and notes, her ransacking Dad's office. "It's that...I'd rather no one but you enter my office when I'm away."

"Okay? When someone wants to meet with you, they should wait out here?"

This was stupid.

What am I paranoid about?

There probably wasn't an extensive list of people in Maker's Mark who my father screwed.

"No." I shook my head. "I'm sorry. Nothing's wrong. Did you call for Aunt Rachel?"

"Yes. As soon as she arrives, Millie will let her know."

Fin

Lacy's tests made me late to the film room. She ordered x-rays, straight on and lateral, and a CT scan, which she said would be more diagnostic. If that was the case, I wondered why we wasted time with the x-ray. I wasn't the only player late. The trainers were passing out x-rays like beads on Mardi Gras.

Results...no—not yet.

"Come back before lunch," she told me. "I'll know more."

"Lacy, you're a godsend to the team, but I know my body. I'm beat up but fine."

"Fin, I believe you. Let's find out what the imaging shows."

The entrance to the film room was in the front,

making it impossible to sneak in late. As I stepped inside, most of the team as well as coaches had their eyes on me. I feigned a smile. "What can I say, Lacy Reynolds wouldn't let me leave."

"Take a seat, Graham," Tilson said, before going back to talking to the team.

I took a seat in the second row near Dennison, Ortiz, and Morgan.

"As I was saying, we had five penalties called on us yesterday. I know that stadium was loud. That's not an excuse. Listen to the cadence. Don't jump early. And the holding calls" —he shook his head— "don't get caught. I'd tell you not to do it. Statistically, more holds go uncalled than called. However, if we piss off an official, they'll be blowing every whistle. I'm saying it. Don't hold."

The examination of the film from yesterday's game went on for a few hours. Tilson did most of the talking, but Coaches Pratt and Brown interjected their thoughts. As the time ran closer to noon, Tilson stepped forward.

"As you're aware, Mr. Hubbard's service is tomorrow at eleven. It's going to be here in the inside practice facility. Everyone on the team has been invited. You should have already informed Mr. Hubbard's office of your attendance. If you haven't, do it. By no means is attendance mandatory. Participation is up to you. There will be a strict no-phone policy. No cameras. No recording equipment. If you bring a spouse or guest, that policy applies to them too. All phones will be confiscated at the door and returned after the service. For that reason, there will be security present, including a metal detector."

He took a breath.

"Ms. Hubbard is adamant that no reporters attend the service. This is for those of us who knew him and those who were fortunate enough to meet him to pay our respects. Once the service concludes, there will be a dinner in celebration of Mr. Hubbard.

"Ms. and Mrs. Hubbard debated about this detail, as they didn't want the Coopers' cooking and nutritional staff to be required to work. The meal is being brought in from an outside caterer. Take Wednesday and Thursday to recover from the first six weeks. Those of you who need medical treatment, the training center will be open after the service and on the next two days. Friday, we're going to meet here and take a look at our next opponent. Saturday, light practice. Next Monday we come ready to take on the Titans. That means full pads on Monday. Any questions?"

I heard Dennison murmur. The man was anxious to get into full playing mode. He didn't say a word. No one had a question. The air was sucked from the room at the mention of tomorrow's service.

"See you after lunch in your position meetings," Coach Tilson said, releasing us.

Troy turned to me. "How's she doing? Ms. Maeve."

"It's not easy. I didn't know Mr. Hubbard. She sure loved him."

Troy forced a closed-lip smile. "It's selfish of me to want to practice."

"Bye weeks are meant for physical and mental recovery," I said, realizing this was only his second year in the league. "It's nice when they come a little later in the season. Once we're back, we have ten straight weeks. No rest."

"Naw," Troy said, "we're not done the beginning of January. The Coopers will be playing all the way to the Super Bowl."

My cheeks rose. "I like your confidence."

"We're headed to the cafeteria," Dijon said, tapping my shoulder.

"I'll see you there. I'm headed back to the training center."

"How you feel?" Jamir asked. "You looked a little dazed when you were lying there on the field. I was glad when they sent you back in."

Standing, I tried not to groan or grimace. "I'd lie if I said I wasn't sore. That's what two weeks are for." I smiled toward Troy. "Besides, it doesn't take too much energy to sit on the bench. That's where I'll be."

Most of the others headed toward the cafeteria. A smaller group of us went the other direction, toward the training facility. Lacy's gaze met mine when I entered. She waved me toward her.

"Come with me, Fin. I want to show you something."

I stood taller, ignoring the sense of dread. "I figured you'd say all is good and let me eat."

This woman was easily a foot shorter than I was, yet I realized she held the key to my future play. Lacy didn't speak as she took me back to one of the exam rooms.

After closing the door, she spoke. "Have a seat. I want to show you what we found." She remained standing. "Are you sure you haven't had shortness of breath?"

"I told you, I'm fine."

"Fin," she said exasperatedly. "Answer my questions."

"After the hit. I was winded. That's all." There was no way I was going to mention the stars. The trainers did concussion protocol in the tent.

"Nothing since that time?"

"No."

She took the rolling chair and sat. We both turned toward her laptop.

"The reason your side is tender," she began, "is because you have a hairline stress fracture of rib number nine. The bone isn't split apart." She pointed at the screen. "Nevertheless, it is broken. The good news is that your lower ribs are what some call false ribs. They don't attach directly to the sternum. They're connected anteriorly by cartilage. They're usually less stressed. No doubt, the cartilage is bruised."

"How long will that take to heal?"

She inhaled. "Full healing will take four to six weeks."

She must have read my expression.

"A fracture like yours isn't considered serious. You'll probably be good to play in two weeks. I hate to give you this power, but you're the judge of your pain. If your pain level isn't high, you'll play sooner."

My mind was going through the season. I didn't care that I was on the bench. I wanted to be out there on the sideline. "Okay, we're not talking IR."

"Injury reserve, no. You will go out on today's injury report as questionable for the Titans."

"That's the only game?"

"Again, Fin, we'll reevaluate. Quarterbacks can take longer because your position requires torso rotation and impact absorption. Take this week to rest. No weights. No running. No practice."

"Our next practice isn't until Saturday."

Lacy bobbed her head. "It's a good time for a bye week."

My thoughts went to Vee. "Has the injury report gone out yet?"

"The coaches and executives have it. They won't release it to the press until later this afternoon."

Shit.

I needed to get ahold of Vee.

"Thank you, Lacy. I'll do everything you say. Should I wrap it?"

"Not now. That may be in our plans for when you're ready to start practicing."

"Anything else?" I asked, standing.

Lacy stood with me. "The CT scan was to check your sternum and organs. You have a nasty contusion on your chest. The images came back inconclusive." She lifted her eyebrows. "That means nothing was detected. However, if you have any symptoms such as shortness of breath, increased chest pain, or pain of any kind that requires medications, come in. We'll look again."

Vee had too many things to worry about. She didn't need to worry about me. That didn't coincide with my Fin's-in-control model. "Is all that on the injury report?"

She shook her head. "Only the hairline rib fracture."

"Thank you."

"Remember, you're not indestructible."

"Believe me, I know." Quickly, I made my way to my locker. Pulling out my leather duffel bag, I searched for my phone.

Without thinking, I hit the call button next to Vee's name. The call went to voicemail. Of course it did. She was busy. While I'm more of a text type of person, I left a voice message. "Hey, Vee. I just left the training center. Good news, I'm fine. Bad news, that SOB fractured one of my ribs, number nine. Trainers say my name is going out in this week's report as questionable. Not sure if you've seen the report. Didn't want you to worry. Fin's-in-control is still the plan. See you tonight." I hesitated and looked around. Fuck it. "I love you. See you tonight"

I disconnected the call.

Tomorrow was going to be rough. A fucking fractured rib wasn't going to stop me from being there for Vee.

CHAPTER 31

Fin's name lit up my cell phone on the conference table, but my attention was needed with the topics at hand. The executive board met this morning with little hostility. Apparently, that was because the other members were waiting for an afternoon ambush. With the exception of Royce Beasley, the same people who met earlier were now sitting around the large conference table in the executive office suite.

"Projections at the beginning of the regular season," Uncle Darin said, "of Coopers' value by the end of the current fiscal year included a twenty-five-percent increase. That percentage is the norm throughout the league, based on future earnings. That percentage has dropped and is continuing to drop since the news of Reid's death."

I had the spreadsheets on my laptop. "This devaluation is a prediction, not a guaranteed trajectory." I met everyone's gaze. "We've played one game since Dad's passing. We won. I checked our ticket sales earlier this afternoon. There hasn't been a decrease in sales or an influx of cancellations."

"You don't understand," Darin said.

Gritting my teeth, I sat taller. Narrowing my eyes, I lowered my tone. "Explain it."

Darin stood, pushing his chair away from the table, slapped his hands against his thighs, and spoke through clenched teeth. "Vee, you can learn this, but not in time to save this season or save us from the fallout." His nostrils flared. "The CEO position needs to be filled. It needs to be held by someone who doesn't require a remedial course in NFL franchises."

I didn't require a remedial course, but saying that was pointless. "What are our coaches saying about morale?"

Darin looked at Grant.

Grant took a deep breath. "The coaches are worried. So is Royce. He's been the general manager since Grandpa Carroll was alive. He's seen transitions and is genuinely concerned."

I made a note to search for new general managers. "Go on. What about Tilson?"

Grant pressed his lips together. "Concerned, Vee. Everyone is."

"I met with Don this morning."

All the eyes around the table turned to me with expressions of surprise.

"We discussed yesterday's game," I said. "While his compliment teetered on the misogynist side, Don said he was willing to give me a chance." I met Grant's gaze. "If you're hearing something different, someone is lying to one of us." I turned to Lip. "Talk about branding. How are sales of Coopers merchandise?"

"Strong. They went up after the announcement about Uncle Reid. Dennison is always a strong seller. Graham has jumped by over two hundred percent since the preseason."

"Well, he wasn't playing for us until preseason. But that's good." I turned to Darin and lifted an eyebrow.

"Jesus," my uncle said as he sat back in his chair. "It's the uncertainty that will sink us. We're now officially in a bye week, a week since Reid's passing. His service is tomorrow. The NFL world is heartbroken; we all are. However, they're waiting for the CEO announcement. The CEO position needs to be filled by a competent person." He went on. "There are important matters at hand. Last year, the NFL moved to allow private equity firms to hold ten percent of the ownership."

"I'm not selling one percent of the Coopers," I said,

"much less ten percent. The Coopers have been a family-owned team and will remain a family-owned team."

"You know Reid wanted to host a Super Bowl."

"I do."

"Reid was considering the equity firm move," Darin said. "There are multiple league-approved firms. The Dolphins are in negotiations as are the Bills. A private equity firm would give us more cash, unlock liquidity. Reid was looking to invest in Lexington's infrastructure to increase our bid for a Super Bowl."

If this was true, it was something else I didn't know. "Let me get this straight. You're saying that everyone is concerned about the Coopers' value postseason, yet you're also suggesting that selling off ten percent of the team is the answer?"

"That's very simplistic," Darin replied. "In a nutshell."

"You're saying that Dad was considering selling ten percent of the team and would do so without mentioning it to me?"

"If you didn't know, he didn't tell you," Grant said. "We all knew about it."

"Aunt Rachel?" I asked.

My aunt inhaled and exhaled. "The subject came up. Just like the idea of expanding Crystal Light, Reid shut it down."

"Rachel," Darin said, aghast. "You must not have been in the same conversation."

"I'm sorry, Darin. I was. Reid would have rather cut off his left foot than sell even one percent of the team. He wanted the Coopers to stay in the family, whether to his children—Vee—or to all of us. The second option was being discussed."

A look at my watch told me it was approaching five thirty. "I've made a decision regarding the CEO position." The room became quiet. "Tomorrow will be about Dad and family. Wednesday, we will meet in the Carroll Room at ten in the morning. The press release will be out before noon on Wednesday."

Uncle Darin narrowed his eyes. "Vee, you aren't considering an outsider to come in as CEO, are you?"

"You realize only the Green Bay Packers have a non-family member as CEO," Grant said. "There are many of us in the room who are qualified for the title."

I forced a smile despite my aching head. "What would make you think that?"

"I've heard," Darin began, "that you've been talking to one of the owners of the Colts."

I had, but that wasn't public knowledge. The Indianapolis Colts were recently put in a similar situation. The owner passed away, leaving the team to his three daughters. After speaking to one, I had a sudden desire for a sibling—nothing I'd ever wished for before. I was navigating ground that the sisters had recently conquered. Their advice was appreciated.

I'd also worked with my new attorney, Tricia Loften. Between her advice and Cammy Wilcox's, I felt confident in my decision. "I've done research," I admitted. "Within the NFL, owner or family member CEOs are common practice. However, there is nothing in the NFL rules against having a non-family member appointed to the CEO position."

"You can't seriously—"

I cut my cousin off. "Tomorrow is about Dad. No mention of the CEO position. As you all know, the service will be held in the indoor practice facility beginning at eleven. The team and guests will utilize the stands. There will be chairs on the floor for family and close friends. If you haven't discussed the number of chairs you'll need with the executive office, do so right away. More than likely, the staff has already begun setting up for tomorrow.

"The dinner after the service will be catered by Dad's favorite barbecue restaurant. I worked with stadium operations and decided that the indoor practice field is big enough to provide space for both functions. Tomorrow, the field will be divided by a curtain. The tables for the meal will be on the other side of the curtain. In case you haven't heard, Dad's body will not be at the service; instead, there will be pictures of him through the years. If any of you want to say your final words to Dad, you can meet Daphne and me at Hahn Brothers' Funeral Home from nine to ten tomorrow."

When no one replied, I nodded and stood, ready to leave.

"Vee," Lip said, "may I speak with you?"

"Sure." I arched my eyebrows. "Come with me to my office?"

Jen was gone for the night, and the front office was dark as Lip and I made our way back to my private office. "What's up?" I asked as the door closed behind us.

"I told Bre that I needed two chairs."

"Okay."

"I'd like Chris to be there with me. He's been my rock."

"Okay." A genuine smile curled my lips. "Were you expecting me to say no?"

Tears filled his eyes. "I was hoping you'd talk me out of it. Tomorrow will be a lot. I'm not sure it's the right time to make another announcement like that."

"Like you have someone special in your life?"

Lip nodded.

"I think it's a perfect time. No one should be alone. I've debated, but I'm going to ask Fin to sit with me. We've already made headlines. Lip, fuck anyone who judges us."

"You don't think it will hurt the Coopers in any way?"

I shrugged. "I don't know and don't care. Lexington is a progressive community despite thoughts of the state in general. The Coopers will survive this."

"I kind of wish..." He rubbed his nose with the back of his hand.

"What?" I asked.

"I wish I'd have brought Chris to the family suite, so he could have met Uncle Reid."

"I have the same regret about Fin. The morning Dad died, I was on my way to tell him about Fin. I wish they'd gotten to know one another." I tilted my head. "Leigh and Hayden know Chris. Have Uncle Darin and Aunt Rachel met him?"

He nodded. "Yeah." He feigned a grin. "Mom said she's working on Dad. Grant knows I'm gay. He doesn't know there's anyone in my life—anyone special."

"Maybe Grant should find his own special person." I arched my eyebrow. "It wouldn't hurt the chip on his shoulder to get laid."

"Daphne's available," Lip said with a scoff.

"Oh," I said, making a gagging face. "What was with the two of them on the plane?"

"I don't even want to guess." Lip smiled. Leaning closer, he hugged me. "Chris and I will be at the funeral home tomorrow morning."

"I'm looking forward to seeing Chris again."

"Have you really made a decision regarding CEO?"

I nodded. "I have. It feels right."

"Do I get any more information?"

I shook my head.

"See you tomorrow."

"Tomorrow."

After Lip left, I checked Fin's text. There was a recent text message, the one I saw during our last meeting.

"DID YOU GET MY VOICEMAIL?"

I SHOOK MY HEAD. The weight of the day's meetings pressed on my shoulders. I hadn't heard his message. Going to my voicemail box, I listened.

"Hey, Vee. I just left the training center. Good news, I'm fine. Bad news, that SOB fractured one of my ribs, number nine. Trainers say my name is going out in this week's injury report as questionable. Not sure if you've seen the report. Didn't want you to worry. Fin's-in-control is still the plan. See you tonight."

I let out a sigh and went to my computer. Scrolling, I found the email from the training facility with our current injury report.

Griffin Graham, QB – questionable. Rib fracture.

Xavien Martin, DE – doubtful. Knee, MCL sprain.

Eric Rhodes, DE – limited participant. High ankle sprain.

Corden Young, OT – out. Meniscus tear.

Ramel Patel, WR, - questionable. Knee, PCL sprain.

A questionable rating meant that Fin and Patel had a fifty-fifty chance of playing in the Titans game. We had nearly two weeks for their recovery. Our offensive tackle, Young, would be missed. I scribbled a note to talk to Drew about the position on Wednesday. Also, our defensive end, Martin. Hopefully, Brown will look into Pickett from the practice squad.

Leaning back, I thought about my decision for CEO. It felt right for where the Coopers were. Standing, I gathered my things to head home; simultaneously, an echo of a knock resonated through my office.

"Hello," I called.

Bre Stanton pushed the door open. "Vee, can I talk to you?"

Fin

I stopped by my apartment on the way to Vee's to grab my suit for tomorrow. On my way to Vee's place, I made a quick stop at the supermarket. While I craved a thick porterhouse steak, my thoughts went vegetarian. Vee needed comfort food to get her through tomorrow. I found a recipe for creamy cashew tomato pasta. With the ingredients secure, I headed across town.

Ethan told me the main level of the Vine was almost normal. The reporters must have given up. Vee had the support of her neighbors. No one would give a reporter so much as a quote about the Coopers' heiress.

After hanging my suit in Vee's closet, I changed my button-down shirt for a Coopers t-shirt, kicked off my loafers, and started my culinary creation. If the beginning of a game reminded me of my dad, cooking brought back memories of my mom. She was never into gourmet recipes. Mom was a meat-and-potato or pasta cook, perfect for two growing football players. I can't remember her ever measuring an ingredient. "You just know," she would say.

When I was first signed to Atlanta, I shared an apartment for a brief time. My roommate was a newly signed running back who also enjoyed cooking. I suppose to anyone watching us play the game, they'd be surprised that brawny big men can also cook.

Back then, I'd call Mom for recipes, and she'd say something like, season the chicken and sauté. If I asked what seasonings, she'd laugh and tell me to use what I liked. I was working on the sauce for tonight's dinner when my phone vibrated on the counter. As if I'd willed her call, my screen read Mom.

"Hey, Mom," I said, answering.

"Fin, I keep worrying about Vee. Is she okay?"

"The best she can be, considering."

"You know your dad and I are so happy you two found your way back together. It just seems this is a rough time."

"Yeah," I replied. "It is. I'm glad she's not alone."

"Did you know she was dating one of the Clarks, you know from Meadow Farms."

"Mom," I said with a grin, "are you spreading Bowling Green gossip?"

"No. Um, I wondered if you knew."

"I did. They're no longer together if that's what you're worried about."

"I'm not. I'm concerned about Vee. I've been reading the sports news. Some of the prognosticators are downright mean about Vee taking charge of the Coopers. They're ruthless."

My jaw clenched hearing that news from my mother. I wanted to keep it from Vee. "I don't know her decision," I said. "But if Vee decides to take the helm, forget what outsiders say. I know she can do whatever she puts her mind to, and the other members of the team feel the same."

"I'm glad to hear that. Fin, I believe in destiny or fate." Before I could respond, she continued. "You signing with the Coopers. Vee. Now her father. You were meant to be with her, to help her. Please take care of her."

"I will, Mom."

"Tell her we're thinking of her. We also hope you'll bring her back here again."

My smile lifted my cheeks. "I'll tell her. We'll see what happens after the season. Tell Dad I said hey."

"Love you, Fin."

"Love you, Mom." I disconnected the call.

It was odd how saying those words to my mother

when I was eighteen felt impossible. Now at double that age, it felt right.

I heard the beep of the security system as down the hallway past Vee's office, the front door opened. Turning the sauce off, I headed in that direction. A fist clutched in my chest at the sight of Vee. Her shoulders drooped and her chin was down, lost in thought.

The woman I loved was carrying the weight of the world on her shoulders. She might hide it from everyone else, but it was as bright as a neon sign to me.

Vee turned, her emerald eyes glassy as they opened wide. It was almost as if she was surprised that I was standing here in her hallway. I didn't speak. There was plenty of time for that. Instead, I brushed my lips over hers, helped her with her jacket, hanging it on the side hook, and opened my arms wide.

Without hesitation, Vee wrapped her arms around my torso and buried her face in the front of my shirt. Ragged breaths caused her body to quake as I held her tight with one arm and smoothed her chestnut tresses with the other. Scooping her from her feet, I inhaled, cradling Vee against my chest as I carried her into the living room.

We came to a stop as I sat, keeping her on my lap. Despite her current vulnerable state, her round ass over my cock had a way of recirculating my blood. After a minute or two, Vee looked up and wiped her nose on the back of her hand.

"I'm sorry."

"For what?"

She shook her head. "I keep it together all day. Maybe you should go to your place. That way you wouldn't have to put up with me."

Pressing my lips together in a grin, I lowered my forehead to hers. "When I said I want all of you, this is part of that."

"It's not fair to you. We just got back together, and I'm a blubbering mess."

I lifted her chin until our gazes met. "You're not a mess. You're stunning, and what makes you even more beautiful, what makes me remember all the reasons I love you, is that you're willing to show me this side of yourself." I kissed her nose. "Maeve Hubbard, thank you for trusting me with the real you."

Closing her eyes, she inhaled. "On my drive home, I started thinking about tomorrow. I want to stay strong in front of...everyone." She forced a smile and stared deep into my eyes. "I know I said for you to leave, but I don't want that."

"That's good, because I'm not going anywhere."

She lowered her chin. "Tomorrow. The seating for the team is in the stands. There will be chairs on the floor for family and close friends." Slowly she lifted her chin. "You don't have to, but I was wondering if you...?"

"Do you want me in the stands?"

Vee shook her head. "The world knows about us. If you don't mind, I would like you with me."

Relief and resolve filled me in equal measures. Vee wanted me with her in a very personal and public setting. "I'll never leave your side."

She laid her head on my shoulder. "Thank you."

Resolve was equally as strong. "No one will get close to you; no one you don't want to speak to."

"Can you keep most of my family away?"

"If that's what you want."

She lifted her head as she wiggled her nose. "Do I smell something delicious?"

"I'm not sure if it's delicious. It's my first time to try the recipe."

Vee's smile outshone her reddened eyes. "I promise, I can cook too."

"We're still in our Fin's-in-control bubble." I tilted my forehead back to Vee's. "What do you want right now?"

"For tomorrow to be over."

"I can't do that. I can take off your shoes, start a fire, get you a glass of wine, and finish making dinner."

"Almost as good," she said with a grin. "Maybe after dinner, we could revisit your stress-relieving methods?" She sat up, her expression sobering. "Wait. What about your rib?"

"My rib will be fine."

Vee jumped from my lap. "You shouldn't have carried me."

"You're not heavy. My rib will mend. And relieving stress is not against the doctor's orders."

"Are you sure?"

Standing, I motioned for Vee to sit on the sofa. Next, I squatted near her knees and removed each of her shoes. "There, wiggle your toes. You'll be feeling better already. Do I want to ask about your day? How was your meeting with Tilson?"

Vee hummed as she did as I said. "It was better than I anticipated. I feel like I'm constantly needing to prove my knowledge, but for him, it went well."

"For him?"

"The football world is filled with misogynistic, chauvinist men. It's not rumor. It's fact. I've been dealing with it since college."

"Funny, because in this home, it seems I've been doing a lot of cooking."

Vee grinned. "I'll have to find some way to make it up to you."

I made my way toward the kitchen and turned the burner on beneath the sauce. Vee followed, taking a seat at the island. As I filled a pot with water for the pasta, I turned, seeing a slight smile on her lips—an improvement from minutes ago. "What are you thinking?"

She shrugged. "I don't really know. I'm amazed

you're here, and you're taking care of me." Her smile dimmed. "I'm sorry I hurt you all those years ago."

"Vee, we've reviewed the film and identified the issues with our earlier play. Now we're looking forward to the next game."

"Is it that easy?"

I turned off the water and placed the pot on the stove. "For now, let's say yes."

"Thank you for the voicemail. I hadn't seen the injury report. I would have been more worried."

"Wine?" I asked, reaching for two glasses.

Vee nodded. "Bre Stanton came to my office as I was ready to leave."

"She did?" I found a bottle of cabernet and set it on the counter. "What did she want?"

"To attend tomorrow's service."

I arched my brow. "I thought everyone from the football center was invited."

"I specifically uninvited Bre the other day." Vee looked down at the counter and back up. "I gave in. I just told her she had to sit in the stands. During the dinner she must stay away from Daphne."

"Did she argue?"

Vee shook her head. "She asked to come to the funeral home. I said no." She looked up as I handed her a glass. "I probably haven't mentioned it, but I'm close with two of my cousins."

"I remember Leigh."

"She's married now," she said. "His name is Hayden. They're good together. I'm also close to Phillip. He goes by Lip."

Taking a sip of my wine. I tried to remember. "He wasn't the one at the meeting about my contract."

"No," she said, exhaling. "That's Grant. Lip is his younger brother. They'll all be at the funeral home, service, and dinner tomorrow. I just wanted to prepare you. Lip isn't married, but he is seeing someone. His name is Christopher—Chris."

A laugh came from my throat. "Did you think that would bother me?"

Vee shrugged.

"If your cousin is happy, that's all that matters." I lifted my glass. "To finally meeting your family."

Vee lifted her glass and we clicked. "It's not all it's cracked up to be."

After we both took a drink, I said, "My mom called tonight. She said to tell you she's thinking of you."

Vee smiled. "That's nice." She tilted her head. "She knows about us...that we're back together?"

"And she's thrilled."

She exhaled. "That's how a family should be."

CHAPTER 33

Fin

I woke up before my six o'clock alarm. Blinking awake, I reached for my phone. Vee and I didn't need to be at the funeral home until nine. There was no sense waking her from her peaceful sleep this early. The ache in my side made me grimace, but the warm body at my side was enough to forget the pain.

After the alarm was off, I reached for Vee beneath the covers. My hands roamed over her exposed soft flesh, which happened to be all of her. I was in the same state. Last night, my tension-relieving technique resulted in a much slower union. We took time to explore one another, securely in our bubble and without the threat of curfew.

Vee hummed and wiggled beneath my touch. Her long hair tickled my nose as her round ass rubbed against me, bringing my cock back to life. I closed my eyes, battling between my body's desire and wanting to allow her to continue sleeping. Her proximity was doing little to help.

Vee rolled as her eyelashes fluttered. "What time is it?"

"Too early. Go back to sleep."

Humming, she curled against my side.

I stared up at the ceiling, analyzing the day ahead. My personal assignment was to keep Vee separated from any distress, or as much as possible. She hadn't come out and told me that her relationships with her cousin Grant and uncle Darin, were strained, but I could feel that strain in the air when she mentioned them. I tried to recall what occurred during my contract negotiation. Something seemed amiss.

Vee's warm hands moved over my chest and down my torso. I reached for them as they made their way to my partially erect penis. Seizing them, I craned my neck to see Vee's face. No longer sleeping, her green eyes stared up at me. There was a rosy glow to her cheeks.

"If you start this…"

She smiled at me with a knowing, sexy grin. "You started it."

"I'm trying to let you sleep."

"Don't."

I sucked in a breath as she wrapped her fingers

around my hardening shaft and moved them up and down. "You're playing with fire."

She leaned forward, peppering my chest with kisses. Her long hair created a veil.

My breathing grew shallower as Vee moved lower. Her warm lips closed over the tip of my cock, her tongue swirling. "Fuck, Vee."

The echo of a pop sound reverberated through the room as she lifted her head. Her grin was gorgeous and there was a spark in the green ember of her orbs. "I think I like fire."

"You're forgetting one thing."

"Hmm?" she questioned.

My palm landed on her spectacular ass with a slap. "I'm in charge."

Leaning down, she took me to the back of her throat. What she was doing with her tongue had me seeing stars. My fingers splayed over the back of her head, holding her in place as my hips bucked.

Another pop as Vee gasped for breath.

Taking my opportunity, I repositioned her, lying her back. Vee's hair on the pillow created a chestnut frame around her beautiful face. Her lips were red and swollen. One kiss, my tongue sought entrance, finding my own salty taste. Green orbs stayed locked on me as she lifted her arms over her head, raising her pert breasts and giving herself to me.

With only the tips of my fingers I grazed her warm

skin. From the inside of her wrists to her shoulders, her collarbone to her breasts, with both hands I circled her waist and hips. Whimpers filled the room as goose bumps appeared in the wake of my exploration.

The green stare that had been locked on mine was gone. Her eyes were closed, lost in thought as she concentrated on my touch. It wasn't enough to feel her; my lips needed to join the effort. I spread her legs and lowered myself, inhaling the sweet scent of her essence. Vee's body shivered with need.

It was my turn to bring her pleasure like she'd surprised me with earlier. My first taste was slow and deep, sweet and enticing. Her hips bucked as my tongue lapped and swirled around her swollen clit. Lick by lick, Vee responded, withering under my control.

My rib be damned.

My control was waning, fading into her chorus of moans and notes of ecstasy. This was more than providing pleasure. I was a man starved for this woman. Like a man deprived of substance, I needed more.

Each drop was a sampling that only whetted my appetite. Vee called out my name as she writhed beneath my unrelenting grasp.

"Please, Fin," she pleaded breathlessly.

I didn't need to hear more. Vee's back arched and her lips formed the perfect 'o' as my rock-hard cock delved into her warm, wet pussy. For a moment, I stayed buried, enjoying the agony of her body's vise grip. Ignoring the ache in my side, I thrust in and out. Lowering my lips, I sucked one of her nipples and then the other.

Our rhythm was faster than last night, yet not frantic. This wasn't fucking as we'd done at the hotel. No, what was happening was the art of making love. It was the ultimate closeness that only two people who trusted one another completely could share.

Her body stiffened and her pussy pulsated.

I wasn't done. "One more."

Vee's lips curled. "Sure of yourself."

"Very."

Pulling out, I encouraged Vee to roll to her stomach and lifted her round ass in the air. She settled on the pillows, while I took a moment to appreciate the masterpiece before me. Her well-satisfied core offered no resistance as she released a loud gasp and my length slid deep inside. Thrust after thrust, I drove deeper.

Claiming.

Vee may be the owner of the Coopers, but today as she was met by person after person, it would be my seed deep inside her. I was the one who knew her like no other. It wasn't only the last few weeks: we had a history of memories.

My fingers blanched as they dug into her hips.

Harder and harder. The friction was addicting. The room filled with Vee's wordless exclamations of ecstasy as she detonated again. Her muscles grew rigid.

My body trembled violently. A growl resonated not from my throat but from deep in my chest as I filled her.

I filled her with me.

I was Vee's.

She was mine.

I collapsed, falling slack over her body, shielding her from what our day had in store. If I could, I'd keep us here forever. That wasn't possible. Lifting myself, Vee rolled, bringing her gorgeous green gaze into full view. I kissed Vee's nose. "Good morning."

Her satiated stare met mine as she nodded and wrapped her arms around my shoulders. Wiggling beneath me, she purred, "I'm going to remember this all day."

"Me too. You're mine, Vee. You can be anyone else, whoever you want to be, but remember at the end of the day, you're mine."

She nodded. "I'm yours."

Begrudgingly, I separated our union.

"Fin."

"Hmm?"

"You're mine, too."

"I am."

CHAPTER 34

Vee

Seeing Fin in a black suit, white shirt, and black tie reminded me of the holiday dance we'd attended so long ago. Today, we were quite the pair, not dressed for a dance; instead, both in our funeral black. Our morning activity gave my body an acceptable outlet for my emotions. Instead of crying, I allowed my body to wind taut like a top, only to spin out of control.

Together, we arrived at the funeral home half an hour earlier than I'd told the others to arrive. Rick Hahn, one of the owners, met us in the lobby with his solemn expression and sympathy.

"Ms. Hubbard, if you've changed your mind, we have a hearse ready and available to transport your father to the football center."

"I haven't changed my mind. Thank you. After the family says their farewell, you can do what needs to be done."

"The mausoleum is ready." He inclined his head. "Most people...I don't want you to later regret not being there as we close the seal."

"Mr. Hahn, these plans are what Daphne and I decided." The warmth of Fin at my side gave me the extra strength I needed. "We appreciate you carrying them out."

"Of course." He looked at his watch. "The rest of your family?"

"I told them to be here at nine. I was hoping for some time alone with Dad."

Mr. Hahn nodded and gestured to two large wooden doors to the side. "Would you like me to take you to him?"

"No." I looked up at Fin.

"Do you want me to stay out here?"

I reached for his hand. "If you don't think it's too odd, I want to introduce you to him."

Fin's Adam's apple bobbed as he wrapped his long fingers around mine. "It's not odd."

Mr. Hahn opened one of the doors.

The large room was virtually empty sans the ornate casket, large sprays of amber roses, and a dozen folding chairs. I tightened my grasp of Fin's hand and took a deep breath. From this distance, Dad appeared to be sleeping.

A nervous giggle bubbled out before I could stop it.

"Vee?" Fin questioned.

I shook my head. "Remember in college how I was into Twilight?"

"Yeah."

"I was just thinking if Dad were a vampire, he could wake up."

Fin squeezed my hand.

Daphne wanted him in a suit. I argued. Dad was a jeans and button-down type of guy. If Daphne wanted to be buried in a tiara, fine. That wasn't my dad.

I won. Dad's shirt was a light tan with the Coopers' emblem embroidered on the pocket. His blue jeans were faded. His hands were folded over his torso, his wedding ring in place.

As we crept closer, it would be too easy to believe Dad was sleeping.

My voice cracked. "Dad, I brought someone I wanted...I want you to meet. I know you've met, but not like I wanted you to." A tear slid down my cheek. "I wish I would have told you sooner. You asked me about Fin, about Griffin Graham. We did date in college. We did more than that." I forced a smile and looked up at Fin, then back to Dad. "Dad, we fell in love at University of Kentucky. We made mistakes and parted ways. You brought him back into my life. I wish I could tell you how much that means to me. I promise I'll be okay.

I'll miss you every day. I'll take loving care of the Coopers. You don't need to worry. And, Dad, I'll love Fin, and he'll take care of me."

I inhaled.

"Mr. Hubbard."

I turned, surprised Fin was speaking aloud. "You can call him Reid."

"Reid." Fin stood taller. "I promise to take care of your daughter. I fell in love with her when we were young and too quick to jump to conclusions. Thank you for signing me, for giving me the opportunity to make things right. Sir, I love Maeve."

Turning, I lay my face against Fin's chest. After a few moments, I looked up, seeing the strain in his square jaw and the moisture in his blue eyes. "Thank you."

He wrapped his arm around me. "Thank you for introducing us."

The door opened as a symphony of voices entered. Uncle Darin, Aunt Rachel, Daphne, and Grant. They all paused for a moment at the sight of me with Fin. Grant's jaw clenched, the muscles on the side of his face pulled tight. It was Daphne of all people who came closer.

"Mr. Graham, I presume." She offered him her hand.

"Mrs. Hubbard."

"Oh please, call me Daphne."

Fin showed his million-dollar smile. "Daphne, I'm Fin."

Daphne turned toward Dad. Her smile dimmed. "Reid. You look like you're sleeping." She laid her hand over his. "You're not snoring." She inhaled. "I wish you were."

Uncle Darin and Aunt Rachel came closer.

Aunt Rachel reached for my hand. "How are you, sweetie?"

"I promised Dad I'd be okay."

She looked up at Fin. "I suspect you're part of the reason she'll be all right."

"If I can do anything to facilitate that, I will."

Aunt Rachel nodded. "I'm Rachel Marsh." She offered her hand.

Fin took it and they shook. "Mrs. Marsh, Griffin Graham."

There was a tap on my shoulder. I turned to see Grant.

"Can we have a minute?"

Taking a deep breath, I shook my head. "No, Grant. Not today."

Fin's hand went to the small of my back. His touch radiated warmth and support beyond the physical boundaries. His endorsement helped me power through the rest of the time at the funeral home.

"Do you still want me to sit with you?" Fin asked as we pulled into Maker's Mark.

"More than anything."

My head buzzed as I spoke appropriately to friends, family, and members of the Coopers. If asked only seconds after I spoke what it was I'd said, I wouldn't have been able to answer.

The half of the practice field devoted to the ceremony was packed with people. I couldn't recall inviting so many people. Music played through the speakers. The Coopers' chaplain delivered Dad's eulogy. It was both sentimental and at times funny. As I sat between Daphne and Fin, he told stories that made us laugh and cry.

By the time it was over, my temples throbbed.

As we all stood, Daphne turned and hugged me.

The move was so unexpected, I stood statuesque for a moment before returning the gesture.

"He was a good husband and father," she said.

I swallowed. "He'll be missed."

Daphne dabbed her eyes. "Every day."

Grant touched her shoulder. "Shall we go to the dinner?"

"Oh yes."

Looking up at Fin, I widened my eyes.

He whispered near my ear, "You need to fill me in on that when we're home."

"I wish I knew."

Fin and I both stood abruptly straight as Preston

came out of the crowd toward us. "I did not invite him," I said under my breath.

Although Preston's lips were set in a straight line, in his tailored suit, he looked like he'd just posed for a magazine cover.

"Preston," I said.

Fin placed his hand in the small of my back. I could almost hear him growling *mine*.

"Vee, I had to come." Preston kept his eyes on me, avoiding Fin. "Reid was a wonderful man. I'm so glad I got the opportunity to know him."

Fuck.

Are we in a pissing contest?

"That's very kind of you." I pursed my lips. "Not to be rude, but this service was by invitation only."

"I called Grant. He made sure my name was on the list."

I inhaled. "That's so sweet of Grant, always full of surprises. Do enjoy the meal." I looked up at Fin. "Shall we?"

"Clark," Fin said with a nod.

"Graham."

The other half of the practice field was filled with round tables and multiple long tables filled with food. We searched for the reserved family seating. The air was filled with the buzz of conversation, soft dining music, and delicious aromas of our meal. Looking around, I saw different members of our team and staff.

Their presence gave me a warm feeling. "Dad would be happy with this," I said to Fin as we settled into our chairs. I introduced Fin to Leigh, Hayden, Lip, and Chris.

Most people were seated as Fin's attention was drawn away. "What are they doing here?"

CHAPTER 35

Vee

I followed Fin's line of sight. My jaw clenched at the sight of Trooper Daniels and Detective Oldson standing near the wall, looking over the crowd. "The fuck?" I asked softly. "Are they security?"

No. Uncle Darin said the Coopers provided security.

"Who?" Leigh asked.

"Those two men." I jutted my chin in their direction. Whatever they wanted wasn't happening at my father's wake. "I know one thing. They were not invited." I stood. "I'm going to tell them to leave. If they don't, I'll have the Coopers' security show them the way."

Fin stood with me and walked by my side. "Gentlemen," Fin said, his timbre growling an octave lower than usual. "This is an invitation-only celebration of life."

"Mr. Graham. Ms. Hubbard," Detective Oldson said with a nod. "We're deeply sorry to interrupt. There's been a development in your father's case."

"What case? It was an accident." I inhaled. "Whatever it is, I'm sure it can wait until tomorrow."

"Ma'am," Trooper Daniels said, "is there a Ms. Bre Stanton here?"

I did a double take. "My father's assistant. Yes, she's here" —I looked around— "somewhere."

"Could you point her out?" the detective asked.

"Why?" Fin asked.

"Mr. Graham, this is official business."

"Again," I said, "this could and should wait for tomorrow."

"Yes, ma'am. It could have waited until it came to our attention that Ms. Stanton booked a one-way flight to California, leaving tonight at 9:08 p.m. It's imperative we see her before she leaves town."

A flight?

Bre hadn't said anything about leaving.

"Ms. Hubbard," the detective said, "this is very important."

I turned toward the room and scanned from table to table. "There she is," I said, nodding my chin forward. "The woman with short brown hair at table seven. She's wearing the black dress with cap sleeves."

"Thank you," Trooper Daniels said before turning and walking toward her.

We watched stunned as the trooper approached Bre and spoke to her. She paled as her expression morphed from grief to shock.

I turned to Fin. "I don't want a scene." Inhaling, I walked to the table. "Bre, please go with these gentlemen. They just want to speak to you." I slowed my timbre. "We don't want a scene."

She was now standing, looking at me with tears in her eyes. "Tell them I wouldn't hurt Reid."

What?

"Ms. Stanton" —the trooper had taken ahold of her arm— "please come with us."

"Not here." I growled. "Everyone come with me," I turned, leading this spectacle away from the spotlight. Bre, Detective Oldson, Trooper Daniels, and Fin followed me to the other side of the curtain. A 5-man rush, hoping to stop whatever play was going down.

Spinning, I faced them all. "Tell me what this is about?"

Detective Oldson stepped forward. "Ms. Hubbard, this is an active investigation."

"Dad's death was an accident."

"No longer. His case is officially a homicide."

I reached for Fin's arm. "You think someone killed my father?"

"We can't discuss particulars with you. I can only

tell you we have enough evidence to arrest Ms. Stanton."

"What? No," Bre cried. "I'd never hurt Reid."

Trooper Daniels began reading Bre her Miranda rights, "Bre Stanton, you have the right to remain silent..."

Daphne, Grant, and Leigh came around the curtain. Grant was the one to speak. "What the hell is happening?"

"Don't let them take me to jail," Bre pleaded. She reached for my arm, her lips near my ear. "Vee, help me."

I turned to Leigh. "You're a public defender; can you represent Bre?"

She nodded. "I can, but what about Cammy? Bre is a Coopers employee."

"Please," I said to my cousin. "Go get Cammy."

Leigh nodded and hurried away.

Grant reached for my arm. "What the hell—?"

Fin gripped Grant's wrist.

Shocked, Grant released me and turned to Fin. "Don't fucking touch me."

Fin let go of Grant's wrist, clenching his square jaw. "Vee doesn't know any more than you do. Let the detective tell us what he can."

"What's happening?" Cammy said as she and Leigh breathlessly came around the curtain. Sizing up the situation, Cammy stepped forward. "Ms. Stanton is an employee of the Coopers. I'm the president of Coopers' legal. What crime is she being accused of committing?"

"Ms. Stanton," the trooper said, "you are under arrest for the murder of Reid Hubbard."

There was an audible gasp amongst those of us watching.

Bre looked at me with wide eyes. "Please, Vee. I would never hurt Reid."

"I-I don't know…" I looked helplessly around at my family. Everyone was stunned to silence. I looked from Daphne to Bre. The rest of my family didn't know what I knew—they didn't know about the affair. My thoughts were filled with questions and uncertainty. I turned to look into Bre's eyes.

She lowered her voice, "I can't go to jail, Vee. I'm pregnant."

Thank you for reading RUSHED. I hope you're loving Vee and Fin and enjoying the ongoing saga of the Hubbards, Marshes, and Coopers. Find out what happens next in SACKED, coming July of 2026.

THE COOPERS:

INTERCEPTED

February 2026

RUSHED

April 2026

SACKED

July 2026

SCORED

September 2026

STANDALONE ROMANTIC THRILLER:

FEAR OF FLAMES

October 2025

STANDALONE ROMANTIC SUSPENSE:

DEFENDING LOVE

June 2025

BRUTAL VOWS:

NOW AND FOREVER

May 2024

TILL DEATH DO US PART

June 2024

BOUND BY A PROMISE

October 2024

QUEENS AND MONSTERS

January 2025

TO HAVE AND TO HOLD

March 2025

NAUGHTY AND NICE - A Brutal Vows Holiday Novella

November 2025

SINCLAIR DUET:

REMEMBERING PASSION

September 2023

REKINDLING DESIRE

April 2022

BLACK KNIGHT

June 2022

STAND-ALONE ROMANTIC SUSPENSE:

LIGHT DARK

Republished 2024

Previously: INTO THE LIGHT and AWAY FROM
THE DARK

SILVER LINING

October 2022

KINGDOM COME

November 2021

DEVIL'S SERIES (Duet):

DEVIL'S DEAL

May 2021

ANGEL'S PROMISE

June 2021

SPARROW WEBS

WEB OF SIN:

SECRETS

October 2018

LIES

December 2018

PROMISES

January 2019

TANGLED WEB:

TWISTED

May 2019

OBSESSED

July 2019

BOUND

August 2019

WEB OF DESIRE:

SPARK

Jan. 14, 2020

FLAME

February 25, 2020

ASHES

April 7, 2020

DANGEROUS WEB:

Prequel: "Danger's First Kiss"

DUSK

November 2020

DARK

January 2021

DAWN

February 2021

THE INFIDELITY SERIES:

BETRAYAL

Book #1

October 2015

CUNNING

Book #2

January 2016

DECEPTION

Book #3

May 2016

ENTRAPMENT

Book #4

September 2016

FIDELITY

Book #5

January 2017

THE CONSEQUENCES SERIES:

CONSEQUENCES

(Book #1)

August 2011

TRUTH

(Book #2)

October 2012

CONVICTED

(Book #3)

October 2013

REVEALED

(Book #4)

Previously titled: Behind His Eyes Convicted: The Missing
Years

June 2014

BEYOND THE CONSEQUENCES

(Book #5)

January 2015

RIPPLES (Consequences stand-alone)

October 2017

CONSEQUENCES COMPANION READS:

BEHIND HIS EYES-CONSEQUENCES

January 2014

BEHIND HIS EYES-TRUTH

March 2014

STAND ALONE MAFIA THRILLER:

PRICE OF HONOR

Available Now

STAND-ALONE YA ROMANTIC THRILLER:

ON THE EDGE

May 2022

TALES FROM THE DARK SIDE SERIES:

INSIDIOUS

(All books in this series are stand-alone erotic thrillers)

Released October 2014

ALEATHA'S LIGHTER ONES:

PLUS ONE

Stand-alone fun, sexy romance

May 2017

ANOTHER ONE

Stand-alone fun, sexy romance

May 2018

ONE NIGHT

Stand-alone, sexy contemporary romance

September 2017

A SECRET ONE

Prequel to MY ALWAYS ONE

April 2018

MY ALWAYS ONE

Stand-Alone, sexy friends to lovers contemporary romance

July 2021

*QUINTESSENTIALLY THE ONE

Stand-alone, small-town, second-chance, secret baby
contemporary romance

July 2022

*ONE KISS

Stand-alone, small-town, best friend's sister, grump/sunshine
contemporary romance.

July 2023

*ONE STRING

Second-chance, enemies-to-lovers, fake-date, little-sister's-
best-friend, forbidden, stand-alone contemporary romance

July 2024

INDULGENCE SERIES:

UNEXPECTED

August 2018

UNCONVENTIONAL

January 2018

UNFORGETTABLE

October 2019

UNDENIABLE

August 2020

WHAT TO DO NOW

Visit Aleatha's store to purchase e-books, signed books, and store exclusive items.

LEND IT: Did you enjoy *RUSHED*? Do you have a friend who'd enjoy *RUSHED*? *RUSHED* may be lent one time. Sharing is caring!

RECOMMEND IT: Do you have multiple friends who'd enjoy my dark romance with twists and turns and an all new sexy and infuriating anti-hero? Tell them about it! Call, text, post, tweet...your recommendation is the nicest gift you can give to an author!

REVIEW IT: Tell the world. Please go to the retailer where you purchased this book, as well as Goodreads, and write a review. Please share your thoughts about *RUSHED* on:

*Amazon, *RUSHED* Customer Reviews

*Barnes & Noble, *RUSHED*, Customer Reviews
*Apple Books, *RUSHED* Customer Reviews
* BookBub, *RUSHED* Customer Reviews
*Goodreads.com/Aleatha Romig

ABOUT THE AUTHOR

Visit Aleatha's store to purchase e-books, signed books, and store exclusive items.

Aleatha Romig is a New York Times, Wall Street Journal, and USA Today bestselling author who lives in Indiana, USA. She has raised three children with her high school sweetheart and husband of over thirty years. Before she became a full-time author, she worked days as a dental hygienist and spent her nights writing. Now, when she's not imagining mind-blowing twists and turns, she likes to spend her time with her family and friends. Her other pastimes include reading and creating heroes/anti-heroes who haunt your dreams!

Aleatha impresses with her versatility in writing. She released her first novel, CONSEQUENCES, in August of 2011. CONSEQUENCES, a dark romance, became a bestselling series with five novels and two companions released from 2011 through 2015. The compelling and epic story of Anthony and Claire Rawlings has graced more than half a million e-readers. Her first stand-alone smart, sexy thriller INSIDIOUS was next. Then Aleatha released the five-novel INFIDELITY series, a romantic suspense saga, that took the reading world by storm, the final book landing on three of the top bestseller lists. She ventured into traditional publishing with Thomas and Mercer. Her books INTO THE LIGHT and AWAY FROM THE DARK were published through this mystery/thriller publisher in 2016.

In the spring of 2017, Aleatha again ventured into a different genre with her first fun and sexy stand-alone romantic comedy with the USA Today bestseller PLUS ONE. She continued the "Ones" series with additional standalones, ONE NIGHT, ANOTHER ONE, MY ALWAYS ONE, QUINTESSENTIALLY THE ONE, ONE KISS, and ONE STRING.

If you like fun, sexy, novellas that make your heart pound, try her "Indulgence series" with UNCONVEN-TIONAL. UNEXPECTED, UNFORGETTABLE, and UNDENIABLE.

In 2018 Aleatha returned to her dark romance roots with SPARROW WEBS. And continued with the mafia romance DEVIL'S DUET, and most recently her Brutal Vows series.

You may find all Aleatha's titles on her website.

Aleatha is a member of PEN America. She is represented by SBR Media and Dani Sanchez with Wildfire Marketing.